The Treasure Map

Tyler Scott Hess

To the future.

Chapter One

A Time and a Place

It was the first day of Christmas vacation, and just like any other ten-year-old boy, Jack Monroe awoke with an extra hop in his step knowing he wouldn't be going to school for the next three weeks.

The air, though frosted outside, smelled like freedom to Jack that morning. Furthermore, the forecast on the radio promised there would be an excellent chance for snow to finally stick on the ground, which would make the perfect start to his holidays.

Jack's best friends, the Santos brothers, were twin boys who lived a mere three blocks down the street. They had promised him they had plenty of extra sleds for him to choose from if he came over to play in the morning, given that the snow did indeed stick as they had all hoped.

Jack could hardly contain himself from the moment he hopped out of his bed, which he had so snugly slept in through what had been the coldest night of the season. He had spent most of his slumber in and out of dream cycles, a series of fanciful visions featuring the building of intricately clever snowmen, sledding with precision down the slopes with the Santos brothers, and hitting his classmate Susie Jefferson in the head with a snowball the size of a grapefruit. His fantastical visions would end with a return home where he would enjoy a simple serving of his favorite drink, a cup of caramel-coated hot cocoa in his favorite red and green Christmas mug, as he nestled himself by the fireplace.

But first, Jack had to get himself dressed if he wanted any of those dreams to come true on that day. After all, a boy of his age wouldn't want his friends, or worse yet - a girl like Susie Jefferson, to see him in his pajamas. Unlike a typical school day, on this particular morning, Jack desperately dressed with such great fury that he wasn't entirely sure how many of his garments were put on correctly. He was almost certain that his shirt was on backward, as it didn't feel quite right, but he had already layered himself with a thick gray hoodie, as well as a puffy blue jacket to top it all off, and there would be no going back after all that fuss.

Jack quickly tossed an orange and brown knitted cap over his scraggly black hair, slid some blue jeans over his scrawny legs, and walked out of the room which he had shared for far too long with his four-year-old brother, Calvin. His pudgy sibling with short, spiky brown hair and freckles, which recently began popping up on his cheeks, had been sitting cross-legged and humming quietly without a care in the world. He had already been up and entertaining himself for over an hour, fervently playing with a set of die-cast cars in the corner opposite of Jack's bed.

Jack had always wanted a little brother, at least as long as he could remember such things, and had begged his parents to get him one for years. Despite his repeated requests, they had somehow managed to only give him two sisters before Calvin finally arrived. Samantha, the second eldest of four siblings, was about to turn eight, and Sadie had just turned six the day after Halloween. When Jack finally got his wish granted, he was blindsided by the realization that he would suddenly have to share his room with *the little brat*, as he quickly began to call him.

"See you later, squirt," Jack told his youngest sibling as he slid out of the room, jaunted down the stairs, and made his way to the front door before Calvin could plead to go with him. No way on earth would his mother have let him take the four-year-old with him three entire blocks down the road, but he couldn't take the chance that she would make him stay around to look after him.

"I'm going over to the Santos' house," Jack explained to his mother as he tossed his snow boots on over his mismatched red and gray socks.

"You haven't eaten breakfast yet," Eira Monroe reminded him.

"It's snowing outside right now," Jack pointed out to her breathlessly, as if she hadn't purposely opened the drapes to enjoy the view herself as she took a break from her spreadsheets to enjoy a sip of coffee. "And it's not only sticking, it's piling up!"

"At least take a granola bar on the way out," Jack's mother pleaded with him. "And be back in time for lunch. Your dad said he wanted to show you something when you get back."

Jack rolled his eyes, but swiped a bar from the kitchen, scurried out the front door, and closed it quickly as he began to hear the faintest words beckoning, "Wait for me!"

He knew what would become of the matter if he didn't get away immediately. Acting just as quickly as his feet could take him, Jack decided to take the long way to the home of Matias and Lucas Santos, darting across Holly Street, swerving around El Camino, and galloping down a hill that led straight to their backyard.

"This is perfect," Jack yelled out to his pals as he approached them.

"I know!" Lucas said, his brother nodding in agreement. "The hill ain't much to look at in the summer, but the first thing we told our mama when we moved here last summer was that it would be perfect for sledding whenever it snows."

"What sleds do you have?" Jack asked the brothers as he watched his breath float away through the nippy air.

"Take your pick," Lucas suggested, his open hand offering dibs to their guest.

Matias, the quieter Santos brother, ushered Jack to the side of the house, where they had carefully laid out a plethora of options.

"We've got your traditional sleds, the ones you see in the comics, if that's what you like," Lucas continued. "And then there are the saucers, which might be the fastest, but you might lose control if you're not careful. I think I'll go with the big black inner tube up there against the wall, but on a nice hill like ours, I don't see how you could go wrong with any of these."

"As long as Susie Jefferson doesn't show up to ruin the fun," Jack muttered.

"I don't know why you have such a beef with her," Lucas said, shrugging his shoulders. Matias shook his head without any more of a guess than his brother.

"She ratted me out to Mrs. York!" Jack scoffed, insulted that they would forget such a betrayal.

"That was the first grade," Lucas reminded him. "You really gotta learn to let those things go. Besides, I overheard her telling Lilly that she was going up to the mountains with her family for Christmas."

"Well, she's lucky then," Jack said as he placed a red saucer with a yellow rim under his left arm. "If I saw her coming this way today, I was going to pelt her with as many snowballs as I could make."

The boys all grimaced as they lugged their sleds up the hill for the first time, thinking back to the last snow when Susie had gotten the better of the boys, tricking them into hitting each other with snowballs while she ducked for cover.

The morning wasted away as they stomped up and slid down the same hill more times than they could count, only crashing into each other a handful of times, which led to no more than three or four injuries. This would not need to be addressed by their mothers until they had all finished for the day.

The sun stood high in the sky, partly veiled by a light layer of clouds, and they knew the snow wouldn't last until the following morning. Still, Jack remembered he would be expected back for lunch and had to be on his way.

"You want something to eat before you go?" Lucas asked as he thought about what his mother might be cooking up for them. "There's always plenty around here."

"Sorry guys," Jack said, shaking his head. "My mom mentioned something about my dad wanting me back home for lunch. Has something to show me I guess. I bet it's lame, whatever it is, but I'll get in big trouble if I don't hurry back. This is not the time of year to risk it."

Jack exchanged secret handshakes with his buddies - which I am not at liberty to divulge - and trudged his way back home, taking the more direct route this time, straight up North Avenue.

"Merry Christmas!" Jack heard a voice shouting from across the way. He was startled, and at first instinct, he began to duck, but he found no place for cover. He quickly realized his mistake.

"What do you want, Susie?" Jack asked, hardly able to hide his derision as he turned around and saw his classmate and neighbor helping her parents pack up their full-size pickup truck for a long drive up to their holiday cabin.

"I said Merry Christmas, weirdo." Susie brushed her hair out of her face and gave him a look that Jack didn't know how to interpret.

"Oh," Jack replied sheepishly, not knowing how red his cheeks were getting, though if he had seen a mirror he would have blamed it on the cold. "Fine then. Merry Christmas. Happy New Year and all that."

Susie smiled. Jack turned away and scowled. The only thing worse than when she was mean to him was when she was kind. He didn't know what he was supposed to do with such behavior. For a moment, he thought about picking up a snowball and pelting her once really quick, but when he turned his head back he could see her still smiling.

"Bah!" Jack muttered to himself as he walked back inside his house. He didn't see his family anywhere, so he quickly shook off his heavy winter coat, slid off his boots, and tossed his gloves to the side, leaving everything scattered about the entryway.

"Mom!" he yelled, but he received no reply. "That's weird. I thought she'd have made lunch for me by now. Mom! I'm home!"

Jack scurried upstairs to see if anyone was up there, but the rooms appeared to be empty. He ran back downstairs to look outside, but the back yard was unoccupied as well. That's when he remembered why he was supposed to be home so soon.

"Dad?" Jack inquired as he slowly opened the door to the garage. He had learned over the years not to sneak up on his father when entering his woodshop. "Where is everyone?"

"Oh, there you are!" answered Joshua Monroe. "Mom took your brother and sisters to the store to pick up some groceries. She left a pot of chicken noodle soup simmering on the stove for you to scoop out a bowl for yourself. But that can wait a minute. I want to show you something first."

"What is it?" Jack asked as his father began to pull out a set of plywood cutouts facing the opposite direction from the boy. "I can't see the front."

"I realize this should have been up earlier in the month, but I've been so busy working, I didn't have time to complete it until now," his father told him as they worked together to turn it around.

"Is…is that a full Christmas train?" Jack asked as the engine appeared, fully painted and lit up with carefully placed Christmas lights.

"For our front yard!" his father grunted as they whipped it around to view the rest of the set. "I've wanted to work on something like this since before you were born, but every time I turned around we were having another kid and changing diapers took up all my free time. But now you're all old enough that I don't have to watch your every step whenever I'm home."

"Is it ready to go outside?" Jack asked as he warmed his hands by the small portable heater his father had set up next to his workbench.

"Think you can lift the caboose?" his father asked, gesturing toward the end of the train.

"I've got it!" Jack replied, grimacing as the heavier than expected decoration leaned up against his face. "I think I've got it," he tried to assure himself as they tried to avoid smacking the garage door hanging above their heads.

"Careful now," his father told him as they sidestepped the train out onto the front yard. They set it down with only a little discomfort before Jack ran toward the garage to plug in the lights.

"Is it working?" Jack soon shouted as he traipsed back to the front of the yard.

"Well…" his father said, scratching his head. "Hard to tell in the daylight, isn't it? The lights are on, to be sure, but it's not much to look at just yet. Guess we should get some of that soup and wait until the sun goes down in a few hours."

"Looks nice, Mr. Monroe!" they could hear as a car rolled slowly by. "Merry Christmas, Jack!" said the voice.

"Good to see you getting along with Susie Jefferson again," his father said with a smirk. "Wasn't sure how long you two were going to go at it."

"I'm not. Uh, we're not. I mean we didn't…" Jack trailed off. "Whatever, dad. I don't know what her deal is. Girls are…whatever, I'm hungry."

Jack went back inside, scooped himself a bowl of chicken noodle soup, scraped together two peanut butter sandwiches on sourdough bread, and warmed himself by the fire as his father cleaned up his workspace for the day. He turned on the television, and to no surprise, his mother had made sure that holiday movies were playing on a loop all day, and would likely continue to do so until Christmas Day arrived.

"Maybe I should have had a bigger breakfast," Jack told himself as he realized how hungry his morning had made him. The bowl of soup and two sandwiches were quickly consumed, yet he was no less hungry than he had been when he began his meal.

Jack quickly stood up and made his way back to the kitchen to see what else he could eat, hoping something wouldn't take much effort to prepare, when his perked up at the sound of several car doors shutting in a row and his father's voice offering a loud greeting. "Mom must be home. Maybe she can make me something good."

Jack abandoned his intentions to make himself something to eat, scooted back into the living room, and covered himself with as many blankets as he could find. He sat comfortably and waited for his family to come back inside the house while he watched the television, the flames from the fire helping to warm him up from the long morning of sledding with the Santos brothers.

Jack's brother and sisters made their way into the living room, each giving him a worrisome look as they passed, and headed upstairs without a word. "What's their problem?" he muttered as he watched the Grinch explain something about a light not working properly.

"Jack," his mother addressed him with a sigh as she entered the front door.

"Hey mom," Jack said without looking back at her. "Will you make me some…"

"Jack!" she cut him off with a sharper tone before calming herself quickly. "We…need to talk."

Although he was only in the fourth grade, Jack still knew that nothing good has ever happened in the moments after such a phrase as the one he had just heard. He sighed, slunk his shoulders, and pushed himself off the ground.

"This is not acceptable," she told Jack as she handed him a letter from the school district. He knew what was inside before he opened the envelope, but went through the motions of picking out his report card from the first term of the school year.

Jack didn't want to look. He knew it wouldn't be pretty, but he had hoped against hope that the proof wouldn't have reached his mother so soon. His fingers slipped in and out of the envelope as he mulled over a list of excuses. It wasn't his fault. The teachers aren't fair. The other kids are always distracting him. School is boring. He knew none of those had ever worked.

"Open it," his mother ordered. "And explain yourself."

Jack sighed and gave up the idea that a filibuster might save him from this mess. His eyes looked up and down the chart and he hung his head. "I tried…" he started to say, but he knew that was far from the truth.

"If you had tried, you would be doing better than that," she said, more disappointed than angry. "You're a very smart boy, and so creative, but sometimes…"

"I'm sorry, mama, I just get so…" Jack mumbled, knowing he didn't have an excuse that he could back up.

"I know you are," she said. "But sometimes sorry doesn't cut it."

"But mom…"

"Joshua?"

"Yep," Jack's father said as he entered the living room where the two had been standing. He looked at his wife and shook his head. "Come with me, son," he instructed Jack, hardly able to look him in the eyes.

Jack slunk his shoulders as far down as they could go while standing and followed his father upstairs. "What are you going to do?" he asked, knowing that he could be spending his entire Christmas vacation on lockdown.

"I'm not going to do anything," his father grumbled.

"Huh?" Jack asked, but an answer wasn't quickly offered. What did he mean he wasn't going to do anything? That couldn't possibly be true. He had never gone unpunished for a poor report card. His father's grave response and the silence that followed felt so different than the excitement they had just shared over the Christmas train they had put up in the front yard.

The two of them went upstairs, around the corner, and past the bedrooms, then stopped at the end of the hallway.

"Wha…what are we doing here?" Jack asked as his father looked back at him with a furrowed brow.

Without a word, his father lifted his right arm to the ceiling and pulled down a ladder that would lead them to an attic. "Get up there," he said.

"The attic?" Jack asked.

"I said get up there," his father responded gruffly. "I'm not going to tell you again."

Jack scampered up the steps, not sure what his father had intended for him, nor where to place his feet once he got there. The attic was dark and wasn't a place in the house that he had ever given much thought to in his short life. "I can't see," he said in a hushed voice, not sure if what he might say could get him in further trouble.

His father climbed up after him and reached for a barely visible string that turned on a set of rather powerful lights. Jack covered his eyes with his forearm as the brightness overwhelmed him. He beheld for the first time their oft-forgotten storage chamber and quickly agonized over how he could see every spot of dust that had fallen through the years.

"When was the last time you came up here?" Jack asked. "This place has more dust than the Grand Canyon."

"Last Christmas," his father answered. "That's the only time I come up here most years. I store the decorations in here after Christmas each December. Everything else in here hasn't been touched by a member of this family since I was at least your age."

"I can tell," Jack said as he looked around with a mixture of wonder and grief, knowing that whatever his father had for him, it involved this graveyard of family relics. "But why are we up here now? It looks like you already got all the decorations out of here."

"I did," his father grunted. "Which will make things easier for you than if we had done this earlier in the year. I know how smart you are, how well you think things out when you are inspired, but you have no idea what it's like to work hard when you don't want to do it. But life doesn't work like that. Sometimes you have to do things that you don't want to do so you can do the things you care about most. You're going to be spending your vacation cleaning up this attic. And I don't mean some haphazard job where you sweep in circles for ten minutes and call it good. I want everything looking just the way it did before grandpa filled it up all those years ago. Better, actually. You have more free time on your hands than he did."

Jack looked around the room again and tried to hide the growl that naturally came from his stomach. "How am I supposed to do it?" he asked. "I've never done anything like this before. I don't even clean my room like what you're saying."

His father looked back at him and nodded his head knowingly. "Some things you have to learn by experiencing them for yourself.

This is your job until the work is finished and completion of your task will be subject to my approval. You can come down from here to eat, to sleep, and to get cleaning supplies. Nothing else. And I don't want to catch you slacking off."

Jack watched as his father climbed down the steps, then sat on a dusty box as he thought about where to start. This wasn't going to be like some science fair project that he could whip together at the last minute and hope for a passing grade. This was going to take serious work. He suddenly wished he hadn't rushed home after playing with the Santos brothers. That was the last bit of fun he was going to have for the rest of his so-called vacation.

While he thought about these things, a broom and a dustpan jumped up through the hole in the floor and landed next to him, followed by a spray bottle, a roll of paper towels, and a trash bag.

"Let me know if you need anything else!" he could hear his father say.

"A magic wand would be nice," he muttered to himself, knowing that saying it any louder wouldn't make his punishment get any easier for him. "But I guess the broom is a good start. I don't need to get my feet any dirtier than they are already."

Jack began at the spot where he was standing and without much thought or direction swept the space around himself as he began his journey to a clean attic. Although he wanted to scream, he held back. He was still grasping at the thought that perhaps, if he remained calm, and worked diligently, a remnant of a Christmas vacation might remain when he was finished. However, much like when he was in class at school, it didn't take much to distract him from the task. Jack's mind wandered around the room as his broom work became slower and slower and slower until it hardly moved at all.

"A skylight would freshen up the room," Jack thought, having watched a few too many house fixer-upper shows on television with his mother. "These old chandeliers aren't doing much for the aesthetic."

Jack set aside the broom after he realized that it wouldn't do the work for him. He instead decided to rummage through the maze of antique furnishings and dust-laden boxes that filled the attic floor to nearly full capacity.

"Could have been worse," Jack told himself as he dug his way through a dresser to see if he would find anything inside besides long lost sweaters that he thought should never have been in style. "At least dad took down all the Christmas stuff first. That would have taken ages to go through on my own."

Jack, after rifling through the drawers, realized that it wasn't going to be the jackpot he had hoped to stumble upon while sifting through the wreckage of his grandfather's younger years. The house had been with the family for ages, beginning with his father's grandfather, who had built their home with his own two hands, before it was passed along from son to son. Jack's parents moved in when his mother was pregnant with him and he hoped one day it would be his.

Jack went from box to box, wondering if he might find any valuables, some hidden treasure, or at least something cool that his father might have played with when he was a kid. Although technology had grown by leaps and bounds through the generations, Jack was one who thought more about adventure and reckless abandon than the next electronic craze his friends might try to bring to his attention.

Jack's eyes lit up for the first time since entering the attic when he spotted an old rocking chair, which had been tossed up on top of a cabinet in the far corner. It took a bit of a balancing act, as he shifted his weight from one box of suspect sturdiness to the next, but he managed to clasp it with one hand and tug it down before watching it clumsily bounce from one corner to the other and land precariously next to the hole that led to the second floor hallway. Jack himself narrowly avoided a more serious fate, though he somehow managed to roll his way down the pile without hitting anything sharp or pointy.

"That was lucky," Jack chuckled as he hopped back up without the faintest concern for the condition of anything else in the room. After all, he thought, it wasn't like anyone was missing any of this stuff all that much. It had been sitting there long enough that his father hadn't bothered to ask him to keep an eye out for anything specific.

Nevertheless, something specific caught his eye immediately. When he was younger, Jack's mother would read him a bedtime story nearly every night before he could fall asleep. For years, the only books that would entertain him contained heroes that went on daring adventures, climbed dangerous mountains, survived the thickest jungles, and fought swashbuckling pirates. What always fascinated him most was the reward they would receive for overcoming their fears, which was nearly always a treasure of some sort or another. It could have been a bag of jewels, artifacts from a long lost village, or in most cases a chest filled to the brim with silver and gold. He always wondered what it would be like to be the one to reach the treasure first.

So when Jack caught a glimpse of an ancient green trunk, held together with bronze brackets and buried under stacks of faded newspapers, he got a gleam in his eye. It was such a wonderful vision that if one could have seen Jack at the time, they would have thought he had gone mad, but in his heart he hoped to be like one of the heroes he had heard about in those bedtime stories.

Retrieving this intriguing chest, unfortunately, would take even more work than the relatively accessible rocking chair had been. He knew it might take pure grunt work (the thing he least wanted to do in the coming days) to reach his prize. Jack, undeterred, moved box after box out of his way to clear a path to the chest, desperately hoping something valuable would meet him for his efforts.

Sweat dripping from his brow, his lungs weighed down by the dust, Jack tossed stack after stack of newspapers to the side, then heaved the surprisingly heavy trunk over his shoulders. Nothing rattled inside, but he was more careful with the chest than he had been with anything else in the attic, hoping that whatever was inside would have significant worth. Jack then crept his way back to the rocking chair, set the chest on the floor beside him, and whipped the chair around to have a seat.

It was locked. LOCKED! Jack shook it in disgust. He fiddled with the handles and tested the edges. He turned it upside down and let out a sigh of relief.

"The key!" Jack said in hushed excitement, seeing that it had been taped to the bottom. He grabbed it, turned the chest right side up, and turned the key stiffly inside the lock with his eyes squeezed closed until he was free to lift the top.

When Jack opened his eyes to look inside, his heart sank, and he nearly wanted to pound his fists against the floor. No gold inside. Not a single jewel. Silver trinkets and cherished antiques were nowhere to be seen. Instead, he saw a dusty old parchment wrapped up and tied with a thin piece of string.

Still, after all his emotional investment into the treasure chest, he was intrigued enough that he picked up the parchment and loosed from it a set of papers that had dwelled inside for unknown ages. He quickly unrolled them to discover they contained a map with markings of a place of unknown origin and names of unfamiliar locations.

"What is this?" Jack wondered. "A treasure map? Maybe there was something valuable in the chest after all."

He then began to flip through the set of pages that had been tied together with the map to further his investigation. What happened next I cannot tell you for sure, for some insist even now that Jack had merely fallen asleep, while others will tell the story of a vision that had entranced the young boy, and there will always be those who hold tightly to the belief that Jack Monroe had been transported to another time and place and personhood altogether.

Chapter Two

The Vespasian

My name is Niko Monroe. Dust from the infield settles in my lungs as the guard unshackles my wrists. The closest thing to freedom I've felt in months. I shake them off and let them fall to the ground. I clear my throat, but the guard swats my hand back down the instant I try to cover my mouth. It must be the gravy from this morning's breakfast. Swallowing is difficult now. They want us to look like we've been fed well enough leading up to today. They don't want the people to know how the twelve of us, the tortured men and women who will be standing before them shortly, have been treated while we await their applause. They can't know the truth. They can't consider that we've been dealt with inhumanely. They can't think us to be human at all. They don't want us to be pitied on Independence Day.

It wasn't always like this. And not just the olden days when we were powerful in number and prominence. That was before my time and hardly mentioned in approved history books anymore. But when I was a child there was still some hint of decency among the people of

Ariel to what we call the Faithful. Some of them would spit on the ground whenever I walked by, and the brash ones would call me vulgar names under their breath, but at least we were safe from harm for the most part in my younger days. And there was nothing like this.

The guard in charge of me today is a young cadet who is seeing his first action outside of the prison walls. Everything is under tight lock and key inside the menacing gates of Justice Hall. It's been six months to the day since my capture. It was more like a kidnapping than a proper arrest. Without warning, I was stolen from the streets in broad daylight, bound, gagged, and thrown in the back of a military truck. No explanation came my way for days. I doubt anyone noticed. No one ever does. They locked me up in Justice Hall, that rat-infested penitentiary that I was forced to call home. Food was scarce during the day. Rain trickled down into my bed at night.

Then came the trial, if that's what they want to call it. There was no opportunity for defense. There were no witnesses. Only a prosecutor and a judge. I was sentenced to die just like the rest of them.

Most of my fellow prisoners don't get the pleasure of rotting for so long. They have been saving those of us in line for a special occasion. We are not a hidden statistic like so many others. We are a statement. But to this cadet, I'm a terrifying assignment, though his neatly pressed white uniform, decorated with three blue stripes on each sleeve, barely hides the layer of armor that would protect him from anything I could do to him. Of course, he's scared, but only because he believes every word they tell him regarding my crimes against the State. He thinks I've been feigning weakness all this time. I haven't.

Cadet James prods me in the back to inch me forward. I have little choice. It's either comply with his every command or be struck with fifty thousand volts of electricity. Not that I'd feel the pain come tomorrow morning. I know where I'm going. I know what lies before me. Some will say I've been waiting all this time to receive justice. But I'm here to collect my freedom in front of a capacity crowd at the Vespasian, the largest arena in Ariel City, the capital of the State.

I hear nervous whispers in front of me. Some of my fellow prisoners receive more leeway from those who have been guarding them than I have. Not every guard follows the book, or even agrees with our sentence, but none want to lose their jobs. And none of them would be eager to stand in our place if we were to escape. Chatter from the guards grows stronger. They're checking for updates from the watchtower. It's almost time to proceed.

"This is your last chance," I tell the doe-eyed cadet. I hit the ground faster than I expected. The shock hurt more than I expected. I grab for my back as I am jerked up to my feet. I didn't think he had it in him. Cadet James had been hearing me babble for weeks, twelve hours a day, seven days a week. I thought I might have gotten through to him by now. I guess I'm nothing like my father.

I hear the sound of trumpets playing the song of the State of Ariel. The people chant along with "The Anthem of Peace" as it is called. Every line brings a nudge closer to the gallows. Every chorus squeezes us forward. I'm last in line to meet our maker today, but I'd give anything to be first. I can't bear to witness my fellow workers suffer for their crimes. Not everyone is resolved to die like I am. Some of them believe they have work left to do here. I'm not so sure I deserve such an honor.

The song ends and I hear a very young woman toward the front begin to wail. I've heard her screams in the middle of the night from a cell across and down the hall. She's only been in lockdown for two weeks. She hasn't processed it all. Instinct leads me to take a step toward her, but a quick shock in my lower back sends me to the ground once more.

"That hurt," I say, spitting blood from the cut I received on my lip from the first fall. He doesn't flinch. They weren't assigned to us for light conversation. Guards aren't allowed to talk to us with anything but tasers, batons, or guns. Firearms are typically their last resort, but off-limits today, as they have grander plans for us now that the ceremony has begun. There isn't time to round up more victims.

"Ladies and gentleman," I hear a man's voice saying over the speakers surrounding the stadium. "Today is a day of great peace and prosperity for our humble nation. Every day the honorable servicemen of Ariel apprehend more heinous criminals, murderous terrorists such as the ones you will soon witness as they receive their just due. With each passing day, our streets become safer and our homes more secure. Your children and your children's children will grow up to only know a world where harmony is promoted through the glorious wisdom of our most honorable leader, President Shah."

I wish they would have saved the speech until after my part of the ceremony had come to its conclusion. At least I wouldn't have to stand through this vile rhetoric. It's the same speech every year. It's on everywhere. The entire world watches in solidarity with the president's fight against our cause. This is why we do most of our work through an underground network. But the Faithful are never safe. Just look at me, if you can stand the sight. I made one mistake and now I'm here.

"Liar!" a young man shouts from near the front of the line. He screams out when he is hit with electricity and quickly falls to the ground. I can barely see his face hitting the dirt. His guard is a cruel one I had seen near my cell in my earliest days as a prisoner. The young man must have received a double portion from the taser. It works quicker than the baton and doesn't leave bruises. That's why none of us have been clubbed in the past two weeks. They don't want us to be spoiled for the show.

The voice from the speakers stops in the middle of his diatribe. The guards are asking each other why they are delayed. They all want to get home to their families. Independence Day guards are each rewarded with a vacation when their assignments are complete. Everything is paid for by the State as a reward for successfully contributing to our execution. I've overheard publicly that it's considered to be a well-deserved benefit. I've heard in the dark the secret of its terrible necessity. No amount of rest can cleanse their minds from what they are trained to do to us.

Feedback stretches through the hallway as a woman's stern voice addresses the crowd. "Welcome to this year's Independence Day opening ceremonies," she says to great applause. "There has been a slight disturbance with some of our equipment, but please be assured we will get this sorted out and commence in short time. Please, enjoy a refreshment from our vendors while our workers get this technical anomaly sorted out."

The crowd is restless. I crack my knuckles. I can see the sun has been out for some time, and while they're likely worried about sunburns in the stands, it's frigid in this corridor. Maybe it's just me. My hands are pale. Cadet James looks fine. It has to be me. I notice my breathing patterns have changed. Sweat drips down my brow. My throat is dry. Maybe I'm not ready for this. I need more time. I should have done so much more.

The crowd murmurs. Cadet James taps his baton against the palm of his hand. My fellow prisoners look ahead knowing the inevitable is imminent. One of the Faithful falls to the ground, but not by electric shock. It's the same young woman who had cried out earlier, but this time she fainted, I think. The youngest of us all. Barely eighteen when they picked her up. It didn't take long for her body to waste away. They fattened us up this morning, but after going days without water, she's probably still dehydrated. And they dare to call us animals.

"Give her some water!" shouts the young man before her. His guard reaches for his taser, but he hesitates, and ultimately shows restraint when distracted by the tumult of the crowd. Thunderous clapping and stomping of feet echo through this small corridor. A song breaks out among the crowd. It's a ritual they have picked up over the years. It must be time. We are off to meet our maker. It doesn't matter if we're ready. I'm out of options.

From where I stand, I can barely see the man in front, but he hasn't moved a muscle without orders from the guard closest to him. Not just any guard, but the leader of the entire squadron, who runs the prison system as if the president is looking over his shoulder. As far as Captain Johnson is concerned, the man he's guarding is a master criminal, a devious trickster who's getting every bit of what he deserves. He's been accused of so many things within and outside of courts it's hard for even me to keep track of why they say he's here today. But I know which ones are true. I know because I was there every step of the way. And I know that my father sees no shame in his actions, nor his sentence.

Neither do I. But the consequences of our convictions have led us here and that's something I never foresaw while walking under his shadow, though the warning signs were all around. I'm not sure if I thought they'd never catch us, or if the stories I had heard growing up sounded as realistic as they have proven to be, but today is not a day I thought would be in my future. I thought I'd see my hair turn gray at least, but it's just as black as the day I was born.

My ears ring when they turn the speakers back on. President Shah is introduced. He's greeted with a thunderous shout of loyalty. "King Shah! King Shah! King Shah!" they chant. The presidency isn't enough. They want to make him royalty. One day, he might grant their wish.

Shah will feign humility as always, surely greeting them back with his signature smile and wave, soaking in the applause as he waits for them to settle down and take their seats. I've heard him say in interviews that this is his favorite holiday. All politicians I've ever heard have said the same. But we all know the president never takes days off, always working toward his real objective. Every day he grabs for more power, demanding loyalty, rewarding it lavishly, squashing anyone who might get in his way. Today we are the ants underneath his mighty boot.

"Straighten up, you rats!" Captain Johnson bellows beneath the helmet strapped to his chin. He never was one for manners or patience. "You know the deal. We have every bit of information on you. We know your names, your families, your friends, and anyone you've ever met. We keep track of anyone you might care about. Even the ones who haven't taken part in your crimes. You're not going to make it out of this alive, but if you want them to see the light of another day, then you better do everything I say until you're no longer my problem."

That's the kind of speech that got him the job. Not like the cadet in charge of me, who has moved on to twiddling with his taser, likely in hopes he won't have to use it again today. But it doesn't matter to me who is standing at the lever when the noose tightens around my neck. We're outnumbered, weakened, unarmed, and in no way a threat to the twelve guards keeping us in custody, let alone the dozens of armed officers in and around the stadium. There will be no rescue for us today. There will be no revolt. The bloodlust of the crowd will be satisfied for another year until the next dozen stand before them.

President Shah is closing his commencement speech. Every word drips from his mouth like a hungry lion ready to devour his prey. I can imagine my father telling me to keep my eyes looking upward in times like this. I can't help but focus on the dust beneath my feet. I came from this dirt and soon I will return to it.

I've had half a year to think about this day and our sentence still doesn't make any sense. We are not a sincere threat to their political ambitions, security, or thriving economy. We are few, scattered, and without power. The only aspect of their lives that we can affect is their beliefs. That's why they snap us like twigs. They want to rule the people without interference. They don't want us to infect their values. This is why I believe our deaths will not be in vain. I know to my core that the Faithful will overcome by the power of the blood. There's nothing they can do to us to stop what will come.

I take a deep breath and muster up as much courage as I can while those in front of me also must process our reality. We're all in this together, yet each of us is so alone. All we share now is our crime and a stage to hang upon. I hear sobbing in front of me. I hear deafening silence behind me. A dark void is ready to push me out into the light of destruction. I force myself to keep my head up as we await our next command.

"Without further delay," President Shah says as the crowd lifts its voice, bringing an end to his vulturous speech, "Bring out the guilty!"

"Guilty! Guilty! Guilty" they all shout in unison. My father is pushed forward with a baton and the rest of us are ordered to follow in step. The light is growing stronger as I find my way onto the infield. I haven't seen natural light in weeks. I can barely keep my eyes open as I take in the vision of eighty thousand witnesses clamoring for our official condemnation. I attempt to cover my eyes. My hand is swatted down. Cadet James orders me to keep it to my side, but he won't strike me now if he can avoid it. No more delays.

The guards are yelling at us to keep in line, but I can barely hear their muffled orders over the obscenities hurled at us by the masses. I've never heard half of the words they're using, but I can understand what they're saying all the same. People from all over the world come to celebrate this event, but nothing they say can hurt us now. Nothing hurts anymore. The bruised muscles relax and the bones no longer rub raw against my joints. I smell the fresh air and realize this is truly a gift of freedom. I will not be bound by shackles or iron bars or windowless walls anymore. I won't be stifled or blamed or spat upon any longer. One drop and I will feel no more of this pain forever. Maybe I am ready.

My father walks onto the stage as officials scamper to set the proper pieces of equipment in the center of the platform. President Shah stands poised as an onlooker, cherishing the limelight as he is rewarded by the crowd for his successful leadership in the capture of so many enemies of the State. The rest of us follow in like manner, walking to our final destination. It won't be long now.

We are lined up in order of our determined execution, made to stand to the left of our respective nooses, which hang silently from individual stands designed specifically for this occasion. I don't want to know what they spent on this technology. I'm sure funding is easy enough to come by for this event. No one wants to be the one who votes against anything related to Independence Day. I peek around to see my father far to the right of me. I try to get his attention until Cadet James yanks me back in line. Some in the crowd see his actions and affirm his authoritative stance. Others are too distracted by the jets flying overhead. Captain Johnson smiles out of the side of his face.

My father stands up tall and begins to sing a song so loud I can hear it above the crowd. He could always command attention with his voice, but he is quickly silenced with a baton to his back, which scores Captain Johnson applause from the crowd. It lasted no more than five seconds, but I know the tune he was attempting to carry, and it brings me a small amount of comfort. He used to sing it to me as a young boy whenever I was scared. He sang it to me the day they took my mother away from us. I thought her conviction was an unusual injustice back then. Now I see it was an omen of things to come.

I look up at the rope dangling above and to the right of me. It has my name written on it, matching the stitched lettering on my back, the least sophisticated manner of assuring I'm the right man for the punishment. It took six months to prepare me for the noose and it will do its job in the blink of an eye.

I look high into the heavens as I believe my father would want me to do. His advice has rarely failed me. My prayers are cut short as the master of ceremonies approaches the podium to address the crowd. I knew his voice sounded familiar as it echoed through the tunnel. It's Governor Arrigo, a stout man with a heavy word that can be felt in the stomach. He must be thrilled to be able to host this year's spectacle.

"Hobbes Monroe," he says without delay. "Wanted, captured, tried, and found guilty…"

The crowd interrupts with chants of "Guilty! Guilty! Guilty!"

"Guilty," he continues, almost put off by the interference, "of various irrefutable crimes against the glorious State of Ariel, including public decrees of foreign beliefs, development of secret plots of treachery against the President and the State, including the attempted overthrow of the government."

"Guilty! Guilty! Guilty!" they clamor.

"Let it hereby be known throughout the world that these acts shall not go unpunished. The sentence of these crimes shall be carried out by hanging at precisely noon today," he concludes.

I look up to the clock on the scoreboard. *Eleven Forty-Seven.* My father is led up a short set of stairs to the noose prepared for him, but they must get through the rest of our names before they hang us all in unison. They don't want the procession of death to linger. Crowds have proven to become troublesome when the hangings take too long.

Behind my father is an older man with silver hair and a hard chin. He had sat in a cell next to me. He couldn't speak by the time I was thrown in there next to him, and he spent much of his time with his head buried between his hands, but he was kind and often shared his bread when I was hungry. His crimes are the same as my father's. So is his sentence. An old woman I have never seen is next and she might not have made it much longer with or without today's events. I believe she must have spent her entire incarceration in the infirmary. I have heard rumors about how she ended up that way, but clear information is hard to come by on the inside. Whispers prevail.

The young girl who fainted is next. She's short and frail with light and battered skin. Her green eyes force out her final tears. She's visibly shaking and can barely stand on her own. The young man that tried to defend her follows next to his twin brother. Rafe and Wiley are their names. I remember them now. We spoke briefly in the early days of my imprisonment when they still allowed us to all eat in the same cafeteria. It was one of few privileges we had before it was taken from us. Secret murmurs led me to believe the guards feared a planned escape, though it has been about a decade since anyone had successfully fled the prison.

Wiley is trailed by a man who had been sentenced to die once before. He was part of the last successful jailbreak from Justice Hall so very long ago. An underground hero, everyone knows about his famed escape, though the State suspiciously remained silent on the matter altogether. He was picked up last week in a raid and was quickly placed in our company. He's been living on borrowed time and the gleam in his eyes tells me he's handling this better than the rest of us.

Another young woman follows silently. I don't recognize her. She has long brown hair tied back and a stoic face that shows no fear. She's grimacing. No, smiling. Not a big, toothy grin, but a smile of confidence and sufficiency. A stark contrast to the young man standing tall after her. He's still looking for a way out. His spiked blonde hair stands still in the gentle wind as his eyes dart back and forth. If anyone will make a fruitless run for it, I'd guess he would be the one to do so. I won't be giving them the satisfaction.

A middle-aged man and woman stand between me and the brunette. They briefly reach for each other's hands before their guards pull them apart. He whispered something to her that no one else could hear. I can read her lips say, "I love you too." Putting them next to each other in line was an oversight and will lead to someone's punishment.

My attention is altered when I feel a dull prod in my back. The shocks from earlier have numbed my senses, but it's enough to let me know it's my turn. My name is read and listed along with my stated crimes just the same as all the others. Most of us were strangers outside of the prison walls, and many still are after these months of confinement, but our accusers and condemnation are the same. The crowd cheers for our impending deaths as Cadet James urges me to move on with his taser held tightly inches from my spine. I take three steps up to face the noose that has been calling my name since we arrived at the stadium. My legs shake. My throat is dry when I attempt to swallow. My eyes close as I pray one last desperate plea for help.

"And now," says Governor Arrigo, whose microphone wobbles beneath him, before pausing. "Excuse me. And now," he tries again before his podium noticeably begins to shake. A woman shrieks in the crowd, followed by another, then several more join in before the entire crowd is aware of the situation. I feel it beneath my feet and look around me. The guards behind us reach to their belts to draw their more powerful weapons, but the stage is collapsing beneath us. I see the twins kick over the poles holding their nooses and I imitate their strategy. Cadet James pulls out a pistol, but it's too late. I jump off the stage and feel a sharp sting in my feet and ankles. A minor sprain will not be enough to stop me.

The crowd swarms through the exits. I can see pushing and shoving through the corners of my eyes, but I'm focused on one thing. "Father!" I cry out, but he made it no more than ten paces before the captain tackled him, forcing his head down to the ground.

"Run, Niko!" he yells in agony. "Get out of here now!"

Chapter Three

A Drop of Blood

Jack came to his senses and immediately stuffed the pages back together with the map as he heard footsteps getting louder and louder. He tossed them all into the treasure chest just as he saw his father's eyes peek up and into the attic.

"You can come down for supper," his father told him, his voice short and soft. "Put down whatever you're working on, I'm sure it can wait for later."

"I'll be right down," Jack assured him. When he saw that his father had gone, he opened the chest again to figure out what had happened to him. It made no sense. He was sure he hadn't been reading so intensely he had lost his mind, certain that he'd never been so wrapped up in a book that he had forgotten that he wasn't part of the book. But when he examined the pages, it started just the way he remembered it happening, and when he skipped to the end he saw the last line read as if he had written it himself.

Alas, the letter had finished, and there were no more pages to be found in the chest no matter how hard he looked for hidden compartments. After a few moments of desperately looking for any similar letters around the attic, Jack felt compelled to hustle down to dinner, lest anyone should become suspicious. He was rarely late for a good meal, no matter how invested he was in another matter, and there was nothing like mom's home cooking.

"There you are," his eldest sister Samantha said, scolding him as she had seen her mother do so many times. "I'm starving, and you know mommy won't let us eat until everyone is settled in for grace."

"Sorry," Jack said with a put off glare. "Didn't mean to make mommy's precious little princess have to wait five whole minutes for dinner."

"Jack!" his mother sharply rebuked him. "Your punishment is not Samantha's fault, it's yours, so don't act like anyone else's actions are keeping you up in that attic."

"Sorry, mom," he quickly apologized, knowing the platter of chicken wings and celery sticks weren't going to make it to his plate if he kept up the argument. "I didn't mean to…are there any mashed potatoes?"

This was not an unusual manner of conversation when it came to dinnertime at the Monroe household. Siblings argued, parents calmed them down as best as they could, food was nourishing and filling. But as soon as everyone began to chomp their way toward their final bites, Jack's father realized that the eldest of the bunch had mellowed his bickering quicker than usual, and seemed to be staring off into space, or at least toward the attic he had been working on all afternoon.

"Didn't look like you made much headway," he prodded Jack. "Are you sure you don't need some extra supplies? You know you can enjoy your vacation as soon as it's done…as long as it's done properly."

"Properly?" Jack thought out loud. "No, no, I'm fine…I have been…ummm…looking around to see what kind of stuff we have up there. Can't know where to put things until I know what needs to be moved around, can I? How much of that old junk do we want to keep, anyway?"

His father then began to explain to him about why people keep certain things, whether it be because of sentimental or monetary value, and why some items might have weathered the test of time while others would rot. But that wasn't the question Jack wanted to ask, nor the answer that would help him find what he wanted to discover, which was what happened to Niko Monroe and why the letter was left in the treasure chest in the first place.

"Okay, thanks I guess," Jack said half-heartedly when his father finally stopped espousing his critical theory of spring cleaning. "Do you know if there's anything of any value up there? Can I keep it if there is?"

Jack's father was not amused. "Do you really think I'm going to let you keep a pot of gold if you find it? You're up there as a punishment, not to gain some sort of long lost treasure for yourself. Besides, with how much you eat these days, we need all the help we can get to keep the fridge fully stocked. As far as what is up in the attic…I really don't know. I don't remember letting my parents store any of my stuff up there when I grew out of it…I hardly remember them using it at all. I reckon many of the things up there could be your great-grandpa's stuff. Probably some old war mementos and dusty furniture. I'll help you move the heavy items when it's ready to come down. If anything is in decent condition, I might be able to sell it for a couple of bucks down at the antique shop by the lake.

"Wait…great-grandpa was in a war?" Calvin chimed in.

"That's right," his father answered. "I don't suppose any of you have heard much about that, have you? To tell you the truth, there's only so much I know about his experience in the matter. He wasn't much of a talker, and your grandpa didn't seem to have much to say on the subject himself. But when you're older, you'll take plenty of history classes that will talk about one of the most fearsome wars of all time. I don't know how involved your great-grandpa was on the front lines, but I believe bravery runs in this family, and he was surely a hero like so many others."

"Did he leave any kind of...biography?" Jack asked, trying to not sound like he had secret information. "Something to remember him by?"

"That's a good question," his father told him. "And one I don't know the answer to…but if someone is going to find such a thing, it will be you, and I hope you will share it with us if and when you do. Now help me with the dishes, wash up, and get back to work. It looks like you're going to spend quite a bit of time up there in the attic, at least if you continue at the pace you're on now."

Jack slunk his shoulders back down and did as he was told. He was hoping for an evening reprieve from his punishment, perhaps a night of watching a Christmas movie and eating popcorn as they usually did this time of year. As alarming as that letter had been, the thought of losing an entire Christmas vacation to cleaning up an attic seemed unbearable to him at the time.

When he made his way back up to the attic, he decided the only thing left to do was to do what he was actually assigned to do. Perhaps if he got the ball rolling, it might be easier than it looked, and he might be able to get his mind off whatever Niko Monroe nonsense he had experienced earlier.

Jack thought the best strategy would be to make a game of it. He took a roll of masking tape and marked the attic into three sections.

The first section contained the wall that was closest to the trap door that led down to the rest of the house. That would be the simplest, as it had very little in it, considering the door itself occupied most of the area.

Then there was the middle section, which contained most of the large furniture, including a dresser, a couple of recliners that he thought never should have been kept to begin with, and now the treasure chest that contained the map, which Jack felt was calling to him every which way he turned his head. "Forget about it," he tried to tell himself.

Finally, he would be left with the far section of the attic, which was stacked quite high with boxes and whatever else his grandpa must have been able to chuck in there, and was by far the biggest task he had on his to-do list.

Next, he broke each of the three sections into three smaller sections, making the attic look like a tic-tac-toe board. He then decided that every time he completed a section, he would get a point. He needed nine points to win the game. If he won the game, he would be able to celebrate Christmas. Even Jack knew this game was all in his head, but he had to do something to motivate himself to finish cleaning the attic. Otherwise, he would end up kicking dust around for a few days until his parents would decide to find a worse punishment for him.

To make sure the game was played fairly, Jack wrote down the rules on a piece of paper, made a rough sketch of the attic on the other side of the paper, then taped the sketch to the top of the treasure chest so he could see his progress. With a devilish grin, he quickly made a big red "X" over the section that contained nothing more than the trap door to the attic. "That's one gimme point for Jack," he told himself.

"You're giving yourself points?" he heard his father say as his head and shoulders appeared through the hole in the floor. "I hope you've done more than what I can tell from a glance around the room. You know, Christmas is right around the corner, it would be a shame if you were still working on this come Christmas Day."

"I'm just trying to make it interesting," Jack scoffed. "What are you doing up here, anyway? Is it time for bed already?"

"Not quite," his father answered. "You can stay up as late as you want for as long as you are working on this project, and you can get up as early as you can manage, just do whatever it takes to make your deadline. I'm here because I brought you some extra tools and garbage bags to help you. I also brought up a notebook so you can write down anything up here that you have a question about. I'll let you know if anything borderline should be kept or tossed. And no, we don't want any of those old newspapers. I don't know what it was with my old man and those papers. Rubbish!"

Jack took the notebook from his dad and tossed it next to the sketch on top of the treasure chest. He then held out his hands as he was given cleaning rags and spray bottles of various sorts and a swatter in case he saw any living creatures that needed to be attended to along the way.

"If you need anything else, let me know," his father told him.

"Nothing comes to mind right now," Jack said, but only because what he wanted to say would have gotten him into far deeper trouble.

Back to business, he thought to himself as he looked at his game chart and compared it to the disasters spread throughout the room. Knowing he would feel better about himself as long as he was making checkmarks, Jack decided to start work on the part of the room that was closest to the door. One corner held nothing in it other than three stacks of file cabinets that went all the way up to the ceiling. The other held layers of suitcases which he could tell were from an era that made very little sense to him, each piece looking as if it had been made from a very ugly couch, even though more attractive colors must have been available at the time.

All he had to do tonight was decide where to start, knowing he would need to sweep through the first two sections quickly if he were ever going to get through the final third, the area filled to the brim with loads of junk that he wished he could push straight down a garbage shoot, if only one were available.

"S'pose I'll start with the filing cabinets," Jack shrugged as he walked toward the corner, carefully avoiding the trap door. When he opened the first of a dozen drawers, he beheld an array of colored folders carefully labeled from front to back. Each folder contained a solitary map. He flipped through them briefly and noticed they were all efficiently labeled, and might be quite valuable if they were of any rarity and importance. He had seen a television show where several old, grumpy men talked about such things, and he thought to make a note of them to see if his father thought they would be worth checking out. None of them, however, were anything like the one he had found in the treasure chest.

Jack began to whistle as he went through each drawer to confirm that they each had similar files. It took him nearly half an hour, but he knew that would be quite quick compared to the rest of the sections, and was exceedingly eager to make a second "X" over one of the nine sections on his chart. He made one slash across the corner of the page before realizing that the section wasn't completely finished until his father told him what he wanted to do with the files, so he opted against making the opposite slash across the box on his sheet of paper. That counted as half.

"Getting dark," Jack told himself, not because he could see outside, since the only window in the attic was still blocked on the other end by stacks of newspapers, but because he heard the alarm clock, which he had snuck up with him after dinner. "I better take a look through those suitcases and call it a night.

The greens, the browns, the yellows, every suitcase was hideous in its own way, but the worst of them all, Jack thought, would be the orange and lavender one tossed on top of the stack.

Since his job was to clean up this mess, he thought he might as well move forward by taking care of the worst of the worst. He closed his eyes and feared what they might contain. He considered how he might have to go through years of rat-infested laundry, tubes of unused toothpaste, or a thousand more newspapers.

He sniffed for a clue, rather than opening his eyes, and at first, he didn't notice anything at all. But then a hint of something caught his attention…could it be…yes! It was new car smell. The suitcase was empty. Nothing in it. He checked all the minor compartments just to be sure, but there was not a single item to be found in the entire suitcase. It appeared as if it had never been used before.

"I hope this is a good sign," Jack encouraged himself as he set the first suitcase on its end in a manner that he intended to become an organized row. "Yes!" he said again, clapping his hands as he picked up and shook the second suitcase, a green and maroon eyesore that was almost as hideous on the outside, but equally empty on the inside as the first suitcase had been.

"This is glorious," Jack told himself as he heard a racket downstairs. "I'll get another point in no time."

Knock! Knock!

Jack looked down and saw his father poking his head through the trap door once again. "I know I said you could work here as late as you want to, but it is getting late, so feel free to come down and get some rest if you need it. It does look like you've made a bit of progress this time, at least on one side, so I hope you keep it up in the morning."

"I'll be down in a little bit," Jack conceded. "I'm…well…I think I can get this one little section done before bed and I'll feel better about the whole situation come morning time."

"Fair enough," his father said. "Mom said breakfast is at seven, so you better be up for it if you want to eat before it's all gone."

Jack did not like the sound of missing breakfast. At least not when his mom went to the trouble of making a real breakfast. Bacon and eggs and french toast and pancakes and…well, just the thought of it all made him want to shut down for the night.

"No!" Jack reminded himself. "I can do this. I'm not going to spend my entire Christmas vacation locked up in this filthy old attic like some forgotten creature." He proceeded to flip through the rest of the suitcases with vigor, looking through every nook and cranny that they had available, then lining them up all in two rows as if they were a properly drilled marching company.

"All those suitcases," Jack shook his head as he walked down the ladder to the second floor, "and not a single useful thing in any of them. Maybe gramps had the common sense to not be seen with them."

Jack slept well that night. So well, in fact, that when he awoke he was surprised that his eyes opened without hesitation. He didn't yawn or stretch or gripe about the cold weather. He simply scooted his feet into his slippers and trotted downstairs to where his mother was all alone in the kitchen.

"You're up early, dear," she told him. "Couldn't sleep?"

"Slept just fine," he said. "Maybe the thought of breakfast woke me up."

"Yeah, that sounds more like you," she said, trying to not let him see her roll her eyes. "Your dad says you made a bit of progress on your little assignment."

"Little assignment?" he scoffed. "You mean my punishment for not paying attention to a bunch of boring old teachers? I got a few things done. But that's a big attic. And I don't know what to do with all the junk I've been finding. It is mostly garbage, you know. I found four filing cabinets with nothing but old maps and two dozen suitcases that never found their way toward a vacation."

"That sounds like my old man," Joshua Monroe said as he walked in the room. He sat down next to his son and poured himself a cup of coffee from the pitcher on the table. "Your grandpa always dreamed of adventure. He talked constantly about exploring jungles and climbing mountains. All he ever did was work his hands to the bone trying to make ends meet so your uncles and I could have food on the table. He did pretty well for himself under the circumstances, but he never felt comfortable spending his savings on some wild excursion."

Jack slumped down in his chair and waited for breakfast. He knew he wasn't going to receive any sympathy talking about hard work around his father. He thought he might have been able to eke out some pity from his mother while he had her alone, but that hope had quickly vanished.

"So what should I do with all that old junk?" Jack asked.

"Make a note of it as I told you," his father reminded him. "I'll come up and get the big stuff whenever you're taking a break, and I'll let you know what to throw away when it comes to the little stuff. Just remember…those newspapers have all got to go."

"You sure don't like those newspapers, do you?" Jack chuckled as his mother served him a plate filled with all the foods he woke up dreaming about. "What did they ever do to you?"

His father shook his head and looked up to the ceiling as if he could see through the floorboards straight into the heavens. "Grandpa was always holding onto those things as if they had some significance beyond the events of the day. He thought they were important, but in reality they were always a waste of space. Then when my folks moved out, he refused to take them with him! He said they belonged here. He was a smart man, and a hard-working man, but sometimes…well, I don't know what he was thinking sometimes."

Jack shrugged his shoulders, picked up his empty plate, and set it in the sink to soak. "Guess I'll see you when I see you then," he said with his shoulders drooping a little, still trying to find his way out of having to finish his punishment all by himself.

"You can come down whenever you're hungry, dear," his mother reminded him. "But only to eat. You're not getting out of this no matter how hard you practice your puppy dog eyes."

Jack walked away without another word, then rushed up the stairs before his body language betrayed him. One more roll of the eyes and he thought his punishment might be worsened. He had a decent understanding of when he could push his limits and when it was best to roll with the punches.

Jack made the short climb up to the attic and was immediately brought back to the reality of his punishment. He thought he had made some great progress the night before, having already earned himself three points out of a possible nine, according to the rules he had given himself for a game that only he would ever play. What he had forgotten was that he had started with the easiest tasks possible, and was still staring at a mountain of newspapers and other odds and ends on the far side of the room.

Jack pulled out the notebook his father had given him. He readied his pen and quickly jotted down two notes:

1. Two rows of the ugliest suitcases known to mankind.
2. Drawers filled with useless maps.

"The middle sections don't look like much work either," Jack told himself, trying to gain encouragement where he still could. He looked down at the treasure chest and crinkled his nose. "Maybe I'll find more of that story somewhere among the junk in here. I guess I'll have to wait."

The rest of the morning blew by like a light breeze, which was of some relief to the boy as he dug and scrubbed and fiddled with the few objects taking up what was admittedly the least of his worries. His vacation was going to waste away as he rearranged the bits of furniture in the middle portion of the attic, each piece less valuable than the last.

Jack made note of these objects as well, but was certain that not even a yard sale would be profitable with these broken-down relics. His grandparents, it would seem, did not have an abundance of fancy things to be treasured for generations to come, but rather they kept everything they had just in case they might need them for one reason or another.

"At least I'll have some breathing room to work in when these sections get cleared out," he assured himself. And he was quite right. While he headed downstairs for a bite to eat, his father headed up to remove the heavier objects.

"Leave that treasure chest, will you?" Jack asked his father as he saw him pass by on one of his trips. "I think it's kinda cool, might keep some of my old toys in it or something."

"No problem," his father grimaced as he maneuvered a beat-up recliner through the living room and out the front door. When he came back in he added, "We'll keep those file cabinets for now as well. I think I can use them in the office. Sturdy enough."

Jack finished up his meal and headed back up to the attic for the rest of the day's work. It felt nice having a bit of extra room to sort through the rest of the things. "Six points already!" he shouted, which encouraged him for a moment, before he remembered again that the last three points were going to take days for him to sift through.

Something else was still bothering him as well. Why just the one map in that treasure box and why did it look so different from the others? Why was there a letter wrapped up inside, how did he become a witness of the events it contained, and why did the story cut off so abruptly? And the most curious part of all, why did someone with the same last name as him have such a story to tell? It couldn't be a coincidence.

He thought about bringing it up to his dad, but Jack still couldn't explain to himself what had happened the day before. The story felt so real. He had half-convinced himself that it was nothing more than a dream, probably a result of too much dust in the attic that caused him to pass out and hallucinate, but it was far too clear and vivid.

"Maybe I better look at that letter again," he said, thinking a nice diversion might help him regain some focus for the rest of the day. Jack opened the trunk, and as he had left it, he saw the pages resting just the way he had stuffed them along with the map. He grabbed them with caution, but strangely noticed something that hadn't been there before.

It looked like a drop of blood had splattered onto the map. Jack checked his hands for a moment, but he was sure he would have noticed had he scratched himself. Not a nick on him anywhere. This was a new mark and it wasn't his.

Undeterred, Jack placed the map before him, then set his eyes on the letter, which he would come to find had something new to say.

Chapter Four

Beyond Measure

"Run, Niko!" my father repeats, ignoring the repercussions he would endure from his captor because of his counsel. "Escape!"

His face is mashed against the still shaking ground before he can speak another word. The captain places cuffs around my father's wrists while barking ear-piercing orders at him to stay down. Those might be the last words I ever hear from him. There's no time to think about that now. It's time to heed my father's advice. I need to run. I need to escape this stadium.

But my legs remain unmoved. They are stiff, though stable, and my heavy feet are stuck with indecision and lack of direction to guide them. My neck whips back and forth, guiding my eyes as I look for a clear path for my escape. Cadet James's body is twisted on the short grass covering the dirt floor. His fall to the ground was less than graceful. He pulls his slumping body to his hands and knees, cursing his fortunes. He gathers his senses and looks me in the eyes.

I never should have let him see me. I should have fled the instant my father told me to run. I'm the cadet's only concern at this moment in time. He is one of many for me, but he is the guard who is most alert of my whereabouts, and the one with the greatest consequence if I am able to escape. He reaches for his baton with one hand, then grabs his ankle with the other, grimacing as he shouts words long considered unspeakable, even by those who curse the name of the Faithful. He's not full strength, but letting me go would cost him his job, if not worse. The punishment for losing an inmate from Justice Hall has never been disclosed to the public. I don't think it's because it would lead to a light sentence. As far as the cadet is concerned, it's him or me. For once, I agree with him.

I decide it's unlikely James can run at full strength, if at all. After months of pacing my cell with little nourishment, I'm not sure if I can either, but there's only one way to find out. I don't have to run fast, I only have to run faster than him. There has to be a way out of here that doesn't require prolonged sprinting. I won't win an endurance race. Someone unfriendly will catch up to me. The guard struggles to his feet. He tests his ankle. There's no more time to live in shock. There's no perfect way out. Only God can save me. So I trust my maker and run.

The guard's weapons are useless from long range. Their batons and tasers were designed only for direct contact. Their lack of firearms will be my most precious advantage. We were never supposed to be out of arm's reach, but a disaster like this was not in their plans. He has to catch me himself. I have to make that difficult for him.

The crowds push their way through exit halls like animals escaping a fire, pushing and shoving their way through each other without concern for their surroundings or their companions. I bend my knees and push the dust away from my feet. I'm faster than I should be. I feel the blood blasting through my veins. I reach the wall separating the bleachers from the infield. I leap and push myself up over the wall, but catch my foot on the boundary as I look back to the one who must stop me. I stumble and fall onto the metal floor. I stifle my screams. I know my back is injured, but I won't feel the worst of it until morning. I have to keep moving. Stopping will be the end of me.

I get to my feet and look back to my opposition once again. Cadet James is hobbling toward me, grimacing with each step, motioning to his fellow guards for backup, the dirt on his face unable to mask his pain. Blood and sweat drip from his forehead. His right foot is angled improperly. His face gnashes for vengeance. He blames me for this. I have no time for blame anymore. I only have time for flight.

I look back up to the crowd funneling their way through the corridors to leave the stadium. The ground shakes. Everyone freezes except for me. I can't stop for anything. A smaller tremor reawakens the earth while screams echo through the exit doors. I scramble up the stairs, leaping like a wild gazelle, taking two or three steps at a time until I reach a blockade of bodies. My back could seize up at any moment. I must push through.

I am mindful that the crowd might try to stop my retreat if they become aware of my presence in their midst. They came to this place to see me die today. The State wants them to fear us for their children's sake. But now they're in a place where they are afraid for themselves, not of me, but of the earth itself. I am now little more than an afterthought to these civilians. I sling my sweat-drenched prison shirt over my head and toss it behind me. I'd rather not be seen in my prison number again, though the digits will always haunt me. I can't let anyone else see me wearing inmate number one two two five eight zero again. But the crowd is too distracted to notice anything I do as I work my way past the back of the line, headed toward an exit. They're all trying to do the same thing.

I peek back to see Cadet James reach the boundary below. He realizes that he's too hobbled to make the leap without help. He points me out again to the two guards who have met his plea for assistance. They're older, stronger, and possessing standard rifles issued to officers who guard the prison from watchtowers. An hour ago they would have lost their jobs for pointing their guns at me. Now they're ready and certainly willing to shoot me on sight. I'm wanted - dead or alive. Preferably dead at this point, I'm sure. But they won't shoot me yet. Not here. They could miss and hit an innocent bystander. The press will already have a field day with our delayed execution, but civilian casualties could cause a riot.

I'm wrong. Almost dead wrong. A shot goes by my head and careens off a signpost. I've been too careless. I duck down and with more earnest push my way through the chaos. Cries from the crowd cause a tumult, but no one seeks to stop me. They're all in it for themselves. Thousands of citizens are fleeing the structure without direction or protocol. Terror, rather than pleasure, has temporarily seized their attention. Fear has clouded their already tasteless judgment. I am no longer their chief enemy. I'm their secret companion in flight. They'll worry about me tomorrow when they know they're safe from nature.

The crowd surrounding me scampers left through a corridor, then bend right around a curve, and down a series of stairwells that must lead to freedom. I follow them like a child, knowing only what I'm leaving, not where I'm going. I am among murderers who call me the devil. They have no power over me in this hysteria.

We reach the last set of stairs and scatter to a wider range of options to run. I see open gates with legions flowing through them like a stampede in the wild. Guards attempt to control the flow to no avail. Shaking, I look back behind me. There's no sign of the cadet or any other guards with guns drawn. I look down to avoid all contact with anyone brandishing a weapon.

Gunshots fire. I drop to the ground. Six bullets by my count. I don't know the target, but when I lift my eyes I see a body lying in the courtyard of the stadium. A towering bald man with skin as white as snow has breathed his last. Blood stains the pavement a deep red. I don't recognize the man's attire. I don't know his transgression, but he wasn't one of us. He wasn't me. I'm still alive. I have to keep running. I am one with the crowd who had been so willing to condemn me. They are my unwitting protection. They would have been guilty of my death, but are now guilty of my escape.

Helicopters hover above, guards of the State are shouting muffled orders while their blades deafen the shrieks of the scattered. Are they looking for me? I don't know how many of us might have escaped. Is it just me? Did everyone else suffer the same outcome as my father? It won't be long before every news reporter and officer in Ariel has my mug shot come across their line of sight. I keep my head down and move forward as I consider my options.

The crowd scatters through the parking lot. I blend in with them well enough to keep me safe in their company, but I have to focus to regulate my breath, hoping to overcome the panic that so desperately wants to seep into my skin. I trot at a consistent pace, head straight toward the main exit, not wanting to bring any extra attention to myself. Men and women jet across lanes to locate their cars. I continue without hesitation. I must maintain cover in this chaos. They cannot see my face. They cannot know my name. I cannot return to the hell I've been living in for the past six months.

A siren blares. I nearly trip over the sound, but catch myself on the hood of a car whose driver is not pleased. He yells something unintelligible as I continue my route before he can see my face. The alarm is an emergency warning that no one needs. The entire region would have felt the earthquake. The roads must be cracking. Cars are stalled and traffic is standing still. Motorists honk their horns in helpless confusion. Citizens are safe enough I would think, at least for now, but stranded away from their homes. And I'm still running with only one thought in my mind: *freedom*.

My lungs are heavy as I reach the end of the parking lot. Drivers sit idly by while I pass them unrecognized. Safety officers are glued to their radios. For a moment I almost felt invisible, but I've been spotted by a guard four lanes away from me.

"Stop!" I think he's trying to yell, but I'm not stopping for anything. He blows his whistle. I continue to run. No one is going to listen to him among the sirens and honking horns. "I said stop! No one gets out of here without going through these gates."

I hesitate for a moment as if I'm thinking about how to get away from the man with the badge, but first I want to see if I have reason to fear him. I scan his attire. He doesn't have a single weapon at his side, only a radio to call for help. Still, I look for the best way to dodge him, but I made the mistake of allowing him to see my face. He steps back. He must have realized why I've lost my shirt. If he believes the stories, he'll think I'm a trained assassin. A typical guard from Justice Hall wouldn't know any better. I see him reach to his side, grasping for his radio. Trackers will know where I am within moments. I have to keep going. I can't look back again.

I duck behind an oversized pickup truck and look to flee any direction I can from the guard. I hop over a short chain-link fence I find in my way. I am too weak to fight the impulse to look over my shoulder. The guard slides out of his station to spot me. He knows he can't catch me now, and he must have surmised that I'm not going to go looking for him, but he's still in contact with someone on the other end of the radio. I pray it's no one who can help him.

News travels faster than my feet can carry me. I hear a chopper getting louder. It hovers and searches. I hear screeching over the megaphone. They're all looking for me now. I have to get out of the streets. Too many people can see me out in the open. They know what I'm wearing and that I've lost my shirt. I need to find cover. Most people will think I'm just another lunatic wandering the streets, but trained guards will recognize me, and I have no defense against those with weapons. Maybe they won't shoot me on sight. They might have orders to bring me back to the gallows. I don't like my chances either way.

I see a park in the distance. I think I can reach it before the helicopter can make it that far. I hop across the street while dodging the few cars who have been able to make their way past the guards at the gates. It's a beautiful field, surrounded by trees, like none I've seen in all my former travels. Oaks stand tall with shade and giant green leaves who have yet to lose their luster as summer fades into fall.

I skip over a short bush, stumble on an unseen stone, and land without grace on my ribs. This time the pain I feel is instant. I've never felt so incapable of moving my own body. It will be insufferable tomorrow morning. If I can make it to tomorrow morning. I have to find a place soon where I can heal. And I need something to eat soon. But more than anything, I need water. I'm dehydrated beyond measure. I can't stay here long. I need to come up with a plan or I will perish. I must find a more secure place to hide. Then I have to find a way to escape this region forever. They all wanted me dead today. As far as they're concerned, I might as well be. I can't live here anymore.

I can't move. I think I've broken a rib. Maybe it's only a torn muscle. I don't know how to tell the difference, but I do know I can't take a step without pain. If they catch me, I'm dead. I don't know what will happen if they fail to track me down, but I'd rather rot in a pit than let them have what they call justice. I lie curled up on the ground, with trees blocking the sun from my limp body, praying to God that they won't find me like this. They won't show me mercy if they do.

I feel mud forming from the dirt rubbing against my face as I sob into the shaded ground below. I stretch out my hand from my uninjured left side to cover my tears. I remember my father. I think of his face as he yelled out to me moments before the captain shoved his lips into the infield dirt. But most of all I think about my captivity.

Six months I spent wasting away, counting the days, awaiting my inevitable execution. That's an eternity for one to contemplate life, death, and the way the world works. For me, it was a time to think about what I would do if I were ever released. I never came up with a satisfying answer. I never thought I'd need one. There's no appealing the death sentence for crimes against the State. I'm still not sure I will require any greater understanding of what to do with the rest of my life. The only thing I need to know right now is how to survive the night. Tomorrow will have its own worries.

This humidity is only making matters worse. Dark clouds are moving overhead with the western winds, gray skies building mercifully high above my head, quickly splashing thick droplets down upon my shaking carcass, hiding me from the vultures that would turn me into a meal if I never make another move on this earth.

I have to go. I can't stay like this forever. The guards have surely moved beyond this spot. They won't stop looking until they find me. I'll be on every most wanted list in all Ariel. I can't let that stop me.

I dig my hands into the thickening layers of mud. My ribs stretch with every twist of my body. I cover my mouth with my shoulder and scream into my wretched skin. I can't let that happen again. I must suffer the consequence of pain without sound. I dare not tempt them to find me. I cannot go back to Justice Hall. I'm not sure what I'm supposed to do with my life now that I'm a fugitive, but I know my purpose must be greater than I thought it was when the noose was calling out to me. I have to make my freedom worthy of my father's last name. Hobbes Monroe's legacy will continue one way or another.

Rain washes away any tracks my prison shoes may have left behind me. I see puddles forming in fallen leaves on the ground and make the best use of it possible. I can survive without food, but not without water. I learned that before my incarceration. I never had much to call my own while growing up. I had even less as I traveled from town to town with my father. It worsened with handcuffs and prison bars. I had nothing but what was necessary to keep me alive for the past six months. Rainwater will keep me alive until I find a safe house. Food and shelter will be there. *Please let there still be a safe house.* I must find a village that will overlook my current condition long enough for me to find refuge. I think I remember one where I am headed, just northwest of the stadium.

I bunker myself behind the tallest set of bushes until the sun falls from the city's view. They will search for me through the night, but I have to move sooner than later, and the darkness will be my best chance. If I stagger shirtless through the streets, I'll be as common as the birds in the air or the grass on the ground. The revelry won't stop just because a few enemies of the State have escaped. They fear the

Faithful in Ariel, but not as much as if they were to miss their next drink. This region is nothing if not consistent.

I see the crescent moon peeking over the rolling hills of the city. A full moon would be better. More crazies. More parties. More distractions. I don't have a choice. The sun is setting. I have to move.

My legs wobble. They've done more today than they have since I was first captured. Pushups and pacing in my cell could never replicate years of walking from village to village. I can't concentrate on my problems. I have to focus on my destination. That's what my father always taught me. He always had his eyes set on the prize before him, not the boundaries that could keep him from reaching his goal. Now I have to do the same. I can't rely on him to do it for me anymore.

Breathing hurts my ribs. Every time. My legs are sore and give me problems just standing here in the park. My head is pounding from dehydration. I need more water. My stomach yearns for sustenance. I take a step. I need to remember my goal. My problems are no longer my concern. My destination demands my full attention, though I do not know where I am headed. I must find something familiar.

I reach a path that brings me to a temporary sanctuary. I walk the tattered road. Traffic has wilted. Cracks plague the passage that leads me further away from the arena. The earthquake has done its damage and the ground has settled itself below my feet. No buildings are near enough to assess the grander scale of destruction it may have caused the city. I don't wish danger on anyone, even those who begged for my execution, but I do hope officials are more concerned with crippled structures this evening than they are with my absence. Somehow I doubt it.

A truck comes up to me from behind and I skip off to the side of the road. I stumble through scattered debris, but I find relief when the vehicle doesn't stop to get a good look at me. This happens every few minutes, and every time I fear it may be a soldier's transport scouring the villages, only to breathe easy when they ignore my existence. I must look to them like any other drunk on the street.

I would stay off the road, but this is the quickest way, and I don't have time to waste. I don't know the best route, but I want to see myself out of the view of the city as soon as possible. Villages are scattered throughout the region, too many for guards to comb through every one of them. I'll be protected by the wilderness, but I pray I found a safe house out there. I am a stranger to the Capital, but not everywhere. I have friends. At least I did. I need to find at least one.

City lights come on and I can see the edge of the metropolis from where I'm walking. I see a distant community emerge from the hills with their lights glowing like stars. I don't know which village it is, but I have to go there next. If they don't receive me, I might be reported to the State, but I can't stay out in the wilderness for long.

It's the same with every other unknown village from here. My father took me through all of them over the years. Some were friendly, but wouldn't hear us out. Others were unfriendly, but listened to us speak. Most of the time we would see reactions of a more extreme nature. We faced beatings from callous leadership councils. We were treated to feasts by others. We never took the response personally. It was our message they loved or hated. But the hatred only grew until the day of our imprisonment.

My journey out of the city is wearing on me. Desperate for nourishment, I attempt to find something on the side of the road to eat. I see berries, but it's dark out here, and I can't tell the good from the bad. I'm not foolish enough to tempt poison yet. Nor am I an animal that I would eat grass so easily. But I'm getting closer than I'd like to admit.

City streets have turned into country roads. I know my chances of being recaptured are slimming with every step, but my odds of fainting on the asphalt increase every hour I go without restoration. The nearest village lies flat in a small valley up the hill. My legs scream for rest. My wet shoulders shiver in the moonlight. I can't afford to agree to their terms. I must continue.

Coldness creeps in. Air burns through my nostrils. Drops of rain dampen my socks along the way. I keep my eyes ahead of me, never looking down, never giving in to the thought that I should rest my head on the side of the road. I might never wake up if I do.

I see the village down a slight slope as the road turns around a row of trees. Fog is settling, but lamps glow while debauchery flows through the streets. If I've ever been here, then the work my father and I did here was not well received. My only hope is to find underground believers somewhere.

I see a street sign marking the name of the town. I sink my head. *Welcome to Evansville.* I look back up hoping I misread it the first time, but there's no mistaking Evansville. This isn't just any village. This town was where it all started, not for me, but for my father.

Hobbes Monroe is a hated man in Evansville. And he is beloved. No one is without opinion on the man with the tongue of fire and heart of a lion. That's how he's described here. At least that's what it was like the only time he allowed me to come this far with him on his adventures. He wouldn't let me risk it until I was eighteen. That was three years ago. I don't know what's left of the faithful.

Evansville is the type of town that seems small at first glance, but whose roads wind their way through enough nooks and crannies to make one believe there is more than meets the eye. The good news is that I know where I have to go. The bad news is that I know how I have to get there.

I make a path straight through the middle of the village. Now is not the time to make myself known to this town. I look too much like my father when he was younger, despite my darker skin and longer hair. I won't slip past anyone's eyes if they're sober. There aren't many who will make that a problem, but I keep my head down and avoid interaction.

It does me little good. The people of Evansville are inclined to make their voices known. They are quick to listen, bold in speech, and their judgment…decisive. They believe in right and wrong. They don't agree on who is right and who is wrong. Tonight is not the time for arguments. But that isn't up to me.

"Hey pal," yaps a gregarious man not much older than me. "You look like you could use a cold one."

I keep my head down and don't respond.

"Too good for a drink, buddy?" he continues in sharp contrast to his prior jovial tone. "Get back here. You lookin' for trouble?"

I slip into an alley. I'm too close to lose my freedom now. I can't be seen. I hear him coming. He's shouting words that wouldn't make sense in the daylight. I understand enough to sneak through more twists and turns before he finds me. He's in no condition to chase me. I'm in no hurry to go back. After all, I believe I've found the safe house.

Chapter Five

A Lot to Learn

I hear sirens blare in the distance. My instincts tell me not to run, but to duck out of sight, So I hide behind a large power box next to the safe house. A car drives by within moments. It's a green military truck. State officers are in pursuit. I don't know if I have a bounty on my head, or if they have a reasonable suspicion to search for me out here, but I'm not willing to take a chance I'll go unnoticed. The entire region will soon recognize my face, the mug shot of an escaped convict, an Independence Day disaster. I have to find a way to get inside immediately.

I rise to my feet, check to see if anyone is watching me, then proceed with caution toward the doorway. I stop myself before it's too late. Be smart. If there's one thing I know about safe houses, it's that they're only safe to the ones who belong in them. They're a danger to the unwise and unknowing. I have to remember my training.

My body shivers with a cool gust of wind. The temperature is dropping rapidly. I think about how warm it must be inside, and how much I could eat in one sitting if any rations are left in the cupboards. I hope this place hasn't been abandoned for too long.

Wires have been placed everywhere along the house. Security lines drape the walls. They're mostly a ruse to scare off invaders, cords leading nowhere. There's always a way into these places, but usually only one that isn't set with a trap, and never in the most obvious place. The front door is never the answer. A single knock is enough to set off a series of alarms.

I see a thick blue wire wrap around the left side of the house and think it's likely the active ingredient to whatever might keep me from entering. I follow the line to see where it leads. The building is longer than it is wide, an unusual occurrence in neighborhoods such as this one, but quite normal for a safe house. This obscure building with a rickety front door and a roof that hasn't been restored in decades is a house only the poorest folk would own. Most people would cross the street to avoid it. Most importantly, it will only draw attention to itself if someone cuts an alarm wire when entering. When that happens, it brings harm to everyone involved, but I've been taught all the secrets. Still, I must remember them, and it's been months.

I follow the thick blue wire to the back of the house. What most people don't realize is that cutting any of them will set off an alarm in the house. Disabling them is the wrong approach altogether. But the thickest wires always lead to the real solution. There's always a safe point of entry.

I reach the back of the house and see an unusually large back yard. Safe houses among the Faithful are not known for their vast means.

Odd as it seems, the wire discontinues not in the wall, but far away from the house, and eventually into the ground. I scratch my chin to think. I look up at the fallen leaves covering the tattered roof, but an entrance up there would be too conspicuous for a safe house. The only way has to be through the ground. The wires never lie to the knowledgeable observer.

Every step I take is steady, but cautious and measured. Most of these places are designed for safety, not destruction, but in recent years some wanted criminals were more afraid than others. Some of the Faithful were aggressively afraid. Even after my captivity, I think they went too far, but I am thankful to be aware of the typical traps set up in places like this. I look for danger every time I let my foot touch the ground. I won't let aching feet or a starving stomach be my downfall tonight.

"There it is," I say before putting my hand over my mouth. This is no time to be reckless. Silence is worth more than silver and gold. I caution myself not to run toward the patch of false grass next to the fence. I had nearly forgotten about these underground entries until I saw the wires disappear through the soil. Few of these places are left intact, especially after the mudslides that devastated the hills around the city when I was young, not to mention the raids sanctioned by the State. But this valley isn't steep enough to let the rains sink the town like so many others.

I pull the sod up to see exactly what I suspected. I remove the circular cover, slip down inside before replacing it, and climb down a dozen steps on a rusty metal ladder loosely attached to the wall with bolts that haven't been oiled in ages.

It's dark in here, but there's a faint blue light at the end of a tunnel that leads toward the direction of the house. I don't touch the walls. I hardly want to touch the ground. I don't know the last time someone walked this underground hallway or the last time it was inspected for insects or vermin. I don't know if any more traps are hidden along the way. It all depends on who spent the most time here.

I put one foot out in front of me and wait. I take another step with my torso trailing far behind my legs and wait again. If I set anything off, I don't want to be stuck in a trap. I'd be left to die if anything were to happen. There's no one coming to rescue me tonight, not a soul to save me from my pursuers. There aren't many left among the Faithful.

I make it to the end of the hall before realizing that my legs have started shaking. It's been too long since I've eaten. I don't have much strength in me. I have to ignore my weaknesses for now. I need to climb up the matching ladder on this side to enter the house. I must make one final push to safety.

Every rung is a struggle, my skin clings to my bones, but I reach the top. It's locked. I try to punch it open, but my only reward is a tingling sensation running down my forearm to my elbow. It takes me a minute to regain my composure, my hand now throbbing, my back and ribs tormenting me with every breath. The lid doesn't twist. It won't turn. Of course, it can't, it's a trap.

I jump off the ladder and roll to the side, desperately hoping it's not too late. Within moments the lid slides off and a net drops down.

The floor cover misses my head by a hand's breadth and the net only catches my foot. I close my eyes for a second to steady my spinning thoughts. I want to vomit, but I gather myself before I overreact. I have nothing inside me to lose anyway. And the immediate danger is gone.

I climb to my feet, slide the net off my foot, and pull myself up to the ladder. There may be more traps inside, however unlikely, and I have no other options. This is my best bet. The steps are shaky. I feel a dull pain in my head from where I landed. This will be a long night. I'm not sure I'll make it till the morning.

I heave myself to the ground floor. My head is spinning. I can't take much more of this. I have to find something to eat or I'll pass out. I check my surroundings, but I don't see anyone. I stand up, but not straight, I lean against a wall. Everything hurts now. I hobble into the kitchen. Please let there be food. I'll take anything.

I don't see a refrigerator. There's no time or resources in a place like this to keep cold food. Everything has to be storable for months, if not years. I open the main pantry door. I want to fall. There's nothing here. I check one cabinet, then the next, and one after another until I reach the end of the line. They are all empty. I can't believe it. I'm fading.

I can't stand any longer. I back myself up against a wall, slide to the ground, and let reality soak in. I won't die of starvation in one day. I've been through worse in Justice Hall. At least I'm safe from the State for one night. They don't know about this place. If they did, it would have been torn down by now. They make sure to let neighborhoods know that they don't stand for things like this. They don't use trickery. It's all about intimidation. That's why we always enter safe houses through secret doors in the middle of the night. It's the only way to ensure our protection.

I'll worry about food in the morning. I can't keep my eyes open any longer. It's been...a day. One that I expected would be short and my last. But God gave me another chance for some reason. Another thing to contemplate tomorrow, if I wake up.

I shut my eyes and sleep harder than ever in my life, escaping the physical agony for something exceedingly more dreadful. My dreams are filled with terrible thoughts at night. I see visions of my father's face shoved into the ground. I fear I will always have nightmares of what might have happened after I fled. I hope he's still alive. I pray he still has a chance. I know I'll see him again one day. I don't know if it will be on earth.

When I wake up, I remember where I am, but don't want to open my eyes to see how my body looks in the light of day. I'm too focused on the pain entombed within myself to imagine my outward appearance. Everything hurts, but I reach for my ribs first. I don't know how bad it is, but I know they have to have been bruised from my tumble over the bushes in the park. My head is throbbing, but more from dehydration than from any of the bumps I took during my liberation. I have to find water soon. I force myself to open my eyes, but the second I do I understand I've made a huge mistake.

I catch a hint of light as it breaches thinly shaded windows, then I see a grim face staring at me like a pit bull. An old man with a full gray beard that matches his chin-length hair sits in a hand-crafted wooden rocking chair as he leans up against the wall across from me. The shotgun in his hand appears to be designed for hunting wildlife. Out of instinct, I throw my hands behind my neck, roll down to the dusty wooden floorboards, and plead for mercy. That's how we were taught to avoid instant execution in Justice Hall. It's an action I took on a nearly daily basis before they stopped letting us out of our cells for meals.

"That's what I thought," he says with a soft, tired, graveled voice. "I see you have spent some time in the local pen, young man. Recently, if I'm not mistaken. What did you do? Get busted for breaking into people's homes in the middle of the night? Or is this a new thing for you?"

I don't know if I should answer. My instinct is to stay silent. It was always the correct decision when I was face to face with guards. My crimes are thought far more vile than burglary according to the State. No one is ever executed in Ariel for stealing cash or jewelry. Those are petty crimes according to lawmakers. Dissent is far more treasonous in their eyes. But who is this man sitting in the corner and how did he get in here without me hearing him? I must have slept harder than I ever thought possible. Has he been there all night? Was he here when I entered? I never did clear the house before falling asleep. He could be a squatter or a bounty hunter. We're not the only ones who know how to use trap doors to our homes, especially out here in the hills, where people are prone to have to fend for themselves.

"Answer me, son," he says impatiently, clicking his weapon as he awaits my response. "What did you do? You hurt somebody?"

"No. No, sir. Nothing like that, sir," I tell him. There's something about a loaded gun pointed at my face that makes me extra respectful of my elders. My father always taught me to call everyone sir or ma'am, but I never took him seriously until I learned the hard way in Justice Hall.

"Then what is it? Speak up. I don't have all day."

Neither do I if I don't give him an answer.

"Treason," I confess. "I spent the past six months serving time in Justice Hall for crimes against the State. Please don't shoot me. I've never hurt anyone. I just needed a place to sleep last night. And something to eat."

"Treason?" he asks. "People don't get released for treason. You know, I could go to prison for life just for talking to you. Seems like the kinda thing a fella could get a reward for, turning in a traitor, dead or alive."

I turn my neck to look at him. He isn't smiling. He isn't afraid of what he might do to me. But he isn't sure what to do with me.

"Please just let me go," I beg him. "I haven't stolen anything. I mean no harm. I can't go back there, please. I don't belong in Justice Hall. I don't want to die."

The old man taps his fingers against the side of his gun. He's not set on killing me. He's not set on letting me go so easily either. But his eyes tell me he's got something important weighing on his mind.

"I heard something on the radio yesterday," he says. His tone is grave and somber, like he's telling a story that he doesn't want to share, but must because of the circumstances he finds himself in today. "I listened to the details of an execution down in the city. Independence Day celebration, as you might know. Several of the traitors sentenced to be hung found a way to escape, they said. It must have had something to do with that little quake that shook us up a little in the morning. You wouldn't know anything about that, though, would you?"

He knows. Wait. Others escaped? I'm not the only one who made it out of the stadium. I was so desperate to run as my father had instructed me to do, that I never saw what happened to any of the other convicts between us. I'm not the only one looking for refuge. I'm not in this alone, that is, if I make it out of here alive.

"What did they say about us?" I ask him. I'm into this far too deep to waste time pretending I'm anything that I'm not. Lies are a lost cause among the best circumstances. If this man had an itchy trigger finger, I'd be dead by now anyway, so he must not be threatened by me. I have to squeeze information out of him if I can. I have to know what's happening to them. I have to know what happened to my father.

"So, you are one of them?" he asks, not expecting an answer. "And you're willing to admit it just like that? Are you sure you know what you're doing? You could have just admitted to being a burglar. They don't give out rewards for turning in common criminals. I might have been inclined to just let you go with a warning. But you're not so common, are you?"

"More common than you might think," I tell him. "But less

dangerous than they want you to believe. At least not in the way they want you to believe. Please tell me, I have to know, is anyone dead? Has everyone else been caught? Did anyone else make it this far?"

"Get up," he orders me.

"What?"

"Are you deaf?" he asks, tossing the barrels of his gun over his shoulder. "I said get up, son."

I unwrap my sweaty hands from behind my head and push them at the floor below. They feel looser, but my legs are still bone tired and my ribs still ache like I've been a boxer's punching bag. I grab at the counter to pull myself up, keeping my eyes on him as much as possible to see if he's going to attack me.

"What are you going to do?" I ask him. "If you're going to kill me or turn me in, please at least tell me what happened to the others. I need to know. One of them is my father. They caught him. I know that much. But the others are important too. Even the ones I don't know."

He ignores me as he walks around the corner. It's not like he's afraid of me attacking him. I can barely stand. And he's not afraid I'll run. I wouldn't make it to the trap door in time. But most people wouldn't take their eyes off a convicted traitor in a situation like this. The public thinks we're dangerous, even if they're not sure why the State says we are. He must know something I don't.

The man comes back around the corner and sighs. "Are you going to come over here or what? You're wearing my patience thin."

I look to my left and right before confirming that there's no other option but to follow him, though I'm not sure why he thought I would instinctively follow someone with a shotgun so naturally. But, come to think of it, he didn't look armed when he reappeared. Did he set his gun down so readily? Was it even loaded?

I walk behind him, my knees wobbling a little, my head spinning with every movement. I turn the corner and see him sitting at a table. I was right, there is no longer a firearm in his hands instead I see food on a plate in front of him. And another plate across the table. He's having breakfast. And he's inviting me to join him. I rush to sit down.

"Eat," he tells me between bites. "You've had a long night."

I don't question him this time. I don't even care if the food is poisoned. At least I'll die on a full stomach. No different than what I expected to happen yesterday. Two pieces of toasted cracker are set alongside a bowl of oatmeal and a jug filled to the brim with water. I'm sure I've eaten better food in prison, but this is not the time for standards, it's time for survival.

He lets me eat everything off my plate before continuing the conversation. He never takes his eyes off me, but he doesn't say a word while I restore my vigor. I won't take my time or waste his. I'm too hungry to savor any flavor that might exist in this conservative meal. I'm too thirsty to let a single drop of water go undelivered to my mouth. If this is my last meal, so be it.

The instant I take the last bite of cracker I see a screen turn on in the corner. I didn't think much of it as I was eating, but it is a little odd that there would be anything like it in a safe house. These kinds of instruments are generally considered too expensive and risky. The volume is down low, but the images are unmistakable. Video of the ruined city is captured from helicopters hovering above. They are the same ones that searched for me well into the night, no doubt. Words scroll beneath the images, and though it's been a while since I've had the pleasure of reading, it isn't something I would easily forget. The words are chilling, yet confirm everything I suspected regarding yesterday's wonderful catastrophe.

Six criminals have been recaptured. Six remain at large. They're still searching for us in the rubble. We're all alive, at least as far as the newscasters know, or the State is willing to tell the people, but they're chasing us through the streets. They won't stop searching until they've found us.

"Guess I don't need to introduce myself formally," I tell him.

"I recognized your face the moment you walked in here," he tells me, "but I had to make sure. I didn't know if you were being watched, if you had been followed."

I know I should have been more careful despite my desperation. He was right to consider me a threat, whether friend or foe.

"I had to make sure you are who they say you are, lest my eyes deceived me," he continues. "Otherwise this safe house wouldn't be as safe as it's supposed to be. Strangers shouldn't know the way in. Strangers shouldn't know anything about a house that no one enters or leaves in the daylight. Secrecy is what keeps us safe."

"Us?" I ask, my eyes focused on the screen, but my ears tuned in to what he has to say. "You're one of the Faithful?"

"Of course," he says, picking up my plate to take it over to the sink to clean it by hand. There's no room for laziness or procrastination in a place or time like this. "You think you're the only one who needs a place to hide from the State? We all have our reasons. All our stories start to sound the same after a while. It's only getting worse with time. There was supposed to be another execution in two weeks. I guess they'll double the nooses if they have to. Whatever it takes to keep the people living in fear, to keep them under control."

"Two weeks?" I gasp. "What about the destruction to the city? The stadium was falling apart when I left. People can't even drive their cars in a mess like that. How are they supposed to make it to a tattered stadium for more executions on such short notice?"

The man shakes his head. "We're talking about the State here," he says. "They'll do anything to distract the people from their real problems. That's why they have executions in the first place. They know we're a threat to their control, the power they have over the people, to have them act and think in a way that gives them more power. They can't get what they want if people have free reign over their thoughts and actions."

I never thought about things that way. It seemed so much simpler than that. I believed everyone was against us simply because they didn't want to change. I thought they were lazy in their beliefs. But they're not lazy. They're actively attempting to put us down because they know beliefs are powerful. But I still don't see what harm we could ever do to them by sharing a message of hope.

I look up and ask, "How are we a serious threat to their power? We never taught the overthrow of the government like they say we do.

That's not our purpose at all. You know that. They have to know that."

He shakes his head again. "You have a lot to learn, don't you?"

"Maybe," I tell him. I always thought I'd have more time to learn from my father. But that's not an option right now. "At least I have more time to figure things out. What about the others? Have they released any more information? I need to know what I'm up against. I know I can't stay here forever."

"You're right," he says. "You can't stay here forever. There's only enough food in here for the two of us for today. Then we have to move on to another safe house. I've been here long enough as it is. I think some of the locals have started to notice my presence. I'll take a look at my map and we'll leave tonight. Things are getting dicey in this region. It might be time to move further away from the city."

"Further away? No, I can't do that."

"Oh," he says, furrowing his brow. "And why is that? Do you have a better plan up your sleeve?"

"My plan was to die yesterday," I tell him as I watch the screen display my fellow escapees one by one with all our information and crimes listed for the populace to consume. "I didn't expect to get this far, but I'm not leaving the region without my father. I must find a way to free him, to free them all. Ariel shall not have its brand of justice imposed on my people any longer."

Chapter Six

An Itch He Couldn't Scratch

Jack couldn't believe it. He dropped the pages to the floor, rubbed his eyes, and jumped to his feet, his knees wobbling on the way up. He paced the floor for a minute, scratched at the top of his head, and shuffled the sheets of parchment next to the map. He looked them over quickly, shaking his head in disbelief, but indeed they had changed from the day before. And this time the story was longer. This time it was much harder to recover from what was clearly no hallucination.

"How could this be?" he asked himself.

"How can what be?" his father asked as he poked his head up the attic like a gopher ready for harvest. "Doesn't look like you've done a whole lot here this afternoon. Don't tell me a little bit of hard work is wearing you out so easily."

"Did you put this up here?" Jack asked his father as he wiped the sweat dripping off his forehead, the words escaping his lips before he could think to retrieve them. "Is this your letter? I found it in the treasure chest."

"My letter?" his father shook his head. "I told you, none of this stuff is mine, at least not that I'm aware of. And I don't remember writing many letters, even as a kid, before we had all those fancy gadgets you kids like so much. Why? What's in it?"

Jack looked at the pages again, then back to his father. "Oh, just an old story, I thought you might know something about it," he said, hurriedly putting it back in the chest, not sure what he wanted to admit to his father. If he told him what he thought had happened to him, how the story became so real to him, he might be spending the rest of his vacation in therapy, which sounded like even less fun than cleaning up the old attic. "Thought maybe you did it for school or fun or whatever."

"Doesn't sound like anything I can remember," he shook his head. "Just put it with the rest of the junk. How do you think things are coming along? Looks like you took care of the easy stuff, at least?"

Jack looked behind him and frowned, his mind was suddenly brought back to the reality of his own world and all that he had yet to accomplish. His concern for enjoying Christmas vacation as originally planned had begun to fade away, not only because of the punishment that was taking away his time, but also because of this strange journey he had been taking in the form of Niko Monroe. It didn't make sense to him, and he dared not try to explain it to his family, but it seemed too important to lie to himself as if it hadn't happened twice now."

"Looks like I get to spend some time as a paperboy," Jack grimaced. "Among other things. Say, why am I doing this all of a sudden anyway? Were you reserving this chore for the day my grades got bad enough? I don't remember you ever worrying about the attic before."

"Sounds like you're on to me," his father said gruffly as he sorted through the stacks of furnishings his son had separated to the side. "But no, not really, this was more of an idea your mother and I came up with recently. I know it might seem a bit harsh to you right now, but we aren't making you do this as a meaningless punishment. We need you to learn the importance of hard work. I know that concentrating at school can be hard for you, but you have to learn how to discipline yourself, how to get a job done even when you would rather be doing something else. In the end, I think you'll see that doing hard work has its rewards."

Jack looked again at the stacks of newspapers thrown across piles of boxes and bags of mysterious artifacts that he would get the pleasure of cleaning up in the coming days. His heart, however, was drifting back to the treasure chest behind him and its contents.

"All this stuff up here in the attic has got me thinking," Jack said as his father looked over his notes. "Do you know much about our family's history? I know you said that grandpa never really went anywhere, but what about his father or grandfather? Any cool stories that you know about?"

"Hmmm," Jack's father contemplated. He put his hand on his chin, sat down on a spare chair, and thought about it for long enough that Jack wasn't sure if he should ask a follow-up question or if he was supposed to stand there and wait for an answer. "Your grandpa…he wasn't a very talkative man when I was a kid. He still isn't, of course, you know that yourself, though he did loosen up a bit since my brothers and I went off to college. He used to tell me stories about our ancestors, but I always had the suspicion they were highly exaggerated, might've even been lifted from some books or movies we hadn't been allowed to watch. But I think I might have come across one of those stories by now if they had been plagiarized. Maybe an element of truth belonged to them after all. Curious. Very curious."

"Well," Jack said uneasily. "I guess it's about time for…"

"Right!" his father asserted. "You must be starving. Better get downstairs for some dinner while there's still some left. Your mother made a bunch of those deli meat sandwiches for everyone to dig into. Nothing special, but it should get you through the night."

"Dinner?" Jack gasped. He looked at his watch and couldn't believe what he was seeing. "Dinner? I missed lunch. How could I have missed lunch? There's no way I've been up here…"

"Looks like it," his father shrugged. "Your mother and I were in town for most of the afternoon, didn't think you'd need reminding to grab something to eat from time to time. Guess I was wrong. Maybe tomorrow you should set an alarm so you won't forget."

Jack had had enough lessons for one day. He swooped past his father, scooted down the stairs, and shimmied his way around to the kitchen. The table was empty. Was this some kind of sick joke?

"Yours is in the fridge, dear," his mother hollered from her craft room down the hall. "Everyone else is finished, so eat whatever you want."

Jack stopped listening after the word *fridge*. He didn't hear another word or sound coming from anywhere for the next thirty minutes. He sat at the table, shoved every last bit of meat down his throat, and thought about what was happening to him.

It made no sense. He knew it wasn't a dream. He knew what dreams were like. It wasn't his imagination. His mind never worked like that. Jack wasn't sure what would be considered a vision, but it felt more real than anything he could have ever imagined. He was a part of it. He was experiencing it. The letter…the story…he was living the life of Niko Monroe.

One thing Jack was absolutely sure of was that his body had been worn out. Spending an entire day in the attic, whether he had been awake for all of it or not, had taken his energy from him. He let the food settle in his stomach, then trudged up to his bedroom, where he found his brother, who had long been asleep, the excitement of Christmastime overwhelming the youngest sibling.

Jack slid into his bed, clicked the light off from the lamp on his nightstand, and closed his eyes. He was asleep before he could roll over to his side.

Unlike the night before, this time Jack did dream, and though in many ways it was much like others he'd had in the past, in these dreams he was not entirely himself. His mind was calling back to visions of all he had lived and witnessed as the young man who went by the name Niko Monroe.

Jack mulled over all that had happened to him. He thought about the guards, the impending execution, and the earthquake that helped him escape. He thought it all over and over again as he tossed and turned in his bed. Oh, what it had been like to live on the run, to hide from merciless authorities, and what would cause someone with a death sentence to believe they had been the one who had been wronged. He had never had to consider such things before. Good guys and bad guys were more clear cut in the movies.

When morning arrived, Jack felt more exhausted than when he had fallen asleep and was dreading the day that was ahead of him. He was comfortable with what he had accomplished the previous two days, as he cleared out a good portion of space in the attic, but the final section was the one with the most to organize. It wouldn't be as easy as when he had to sort a couple dozen empty suitcases or flip through a bunch of old maps. He was going to be picking up one piece of junk at a time, looking for anything new and interesting, before almost certainly putting the bulk of it into plastic bags.

Jack did not want to get out of bed. He hardly had a choice when his little brother began jumping on his bed. "Get up, Jack, get up! It's happening!"

Sadie and Samantha ran past his door giggling. Jack had no idea what his brother was yapping about, but he knew it had to be something good, or at least it better be. Jack and Calvin scampered down the steps and hustled through the living room to the kitchen where their mother was busy setting out a bag of flour, a bag of sugar, various little bottles and baskets, and toppings with all the colors of the rainbow.

Jack caught his breath and his heart sank. He knew what all this was for. Every year it was a family tradition for the kids to help their mother decorate the Christmas cookies. The Monroes made sure to produce the same two kinds every year. The first was stuffed with chocolate chips and made according to an old family recipe. The other type was a colorful array of red and green and blue and yellow and white sugar cookies, each color a different flavor of frosting spread carefully on top, then completed with sprinkles spread generously all around the oversized treat. But Jack's Christmas vacation had been taken from him. He wasn't going to be able to take part in this yearly festivity.

His mother looked at him with one eye opened much larger than the other and her jaw clenched like she had just bitten into something surprisingly sour. She looked at Jack's brother and sisters as they washed up and began to tie aprons around their backs.

Jack didn't want to hear the words. He sighed and began to walk back toward the living room, his eyes set on his feet, his mind already working on what was to come his way for the rest of the week.

"Where are you going?" his mother asked him sternly. "Did you really think you were going to get out of helping your brother and sisters with the annual duty of making the Christmas cookies?"

Jack stopped in his tracks.

"They don't make themselves, you know," she said, pointing at the table as Calvin started rolling scoops of dough into misshapen balls and setting them onto a tray for baking. "You're still a part of this family. Get on with it now."

Jack trembled with excitement. He knew it was only a matter of time before all the cookies were baked, and he would eventually be sent back up to continue his mission, but for that brief period he set aside his worries about the filth up in the attic, the newspapers, the garbage bags, and even the visions of Niko Monroe that had mangled his Christmas vacation into a jumbled mess.

Instead, as he intricately placed tiny hard red candies onto a sugar cookie, he thought about how it wasn't so bad having a brother and sisters to share the house with, even if they did steal some of his attention and maybe a few of his presents along the way. At least he wasn't alone. Not when they're around.

But it wouldn't last forever. While his mother assured him that she would save him some cookies and an extra spoonful of raw chocolate chip cookie dough, he would have to head back up to the attic to complete his punishment. Christmas would be here soon, and he didn't want to be spending it sorting through old newspapers.

Nevertheless, Jack dragged his feet back through the living room, climbed his way upstairs, and pulled himself up into the attic.

"I hope the smell improves up here soon," Jack complained. He knew if he could manage to reach the one small window on the far side, then he should at least be able to air it out, but the musty scent wasn't going to dissipate without some help, and the window was still far out of his grasp.

"How about a new game?" Jack said to himself. He lugged up a garbage can to the attic, put a bag in it accordingly, and began to play a version of basketball that gained him two points for every newspaper he could toss into the can, three points if he did it over his shoulder without looking. Even though he had no competition, and no basis for comparison to how anyone else would have done, he thought he was pretty good.

By the time lunch rolled around, Jack had filled four garbage cans with nothing in them but the old newspapers his father had insisted were of no value. He couldn't imagine why his grandpa had collected them, especially since he hadn't bothered to do so in any meaningful way. They weren't well organized, nor were they protected in the least bit, and most of them looked as if they hadn't even been read. They were good for nothing but taking up space in a long-forgotten part of their home.

"How's it coming along there, buddy?" his father asked, his head popping up through the hole once again to check on his son. "Brought you some lunch. Your mom thought you might like some peanut butter and jelly today."

Buddy? That's what his father called him when he was four years old. It took him off guard, especially since he was in the middle of working out his punishment. It didn't seem like they were buddies at all, at least not since his report card made its way home.

"Fine," Jack said. "A few thousand more bits of junk and I might be able to open that window over there.

"Oh, it's not that bad," his father told him.

"Are you kidding?" Jack argued. "I can barely breathe up here."

"Oh, no, you're right about the smell," his father conceded. "I mean you've almost made your way to the window there. If you concentrate on a path through the center this afternoon, I think you'll get there in no time. And once that's done, you'll have a lot more room to move around up here. You should have plenty of time to get it all done before Christmas, as long as you concentrate on your work rate."

Jack pulled up one of the chairs that hadn't been taken to the thrift shop and hoped it wouldn't collapse under him. He chomped into one of the sandwiches his father brought up for him and gnashed it with his teeth.

Joshua Monroe busied himself by tossing stacks of garbage bags, each filled to the brim, down to the second floor below them. As much as it was a punishment for Jack, it had given him something to do while he was home for the holidays as well. He was always a person who couldn't sit still, even when he was supposed to be on vacation, but Jack still thought it odd he would be so eager to help him with the heavy lifting.

"So you never got a bad report card when you were my age?" Jack asked his father.

"A few here and there," he answered his son. "Why do you ask?"

"Just thought if you had gotten a bad report card, you might have been the one to have to clean up this mess," Jack confessed. "Doesn't seem fair."

His father smirked. "Life's not fair," he said, rubbing his thumbs under his eyes. "But I think in the end, you'll see you are the one getting the good end of the deal. It could certainly be worse. Anyway, bring down that plate next time you make your way to the kitchen. Looks like I've got enough newspapers to take down to the recycling center for one day. Let me know if you run into anything special in all this rubbish, will ya?"

"Not very likely," Jack muttered as he began to eat his second sandwich. Of course, by that he meant for his father to not find out about the map and the rest of the pages he had been finding in the green treasure chest that had been staring at him all morning. He wasn't sure exactly why he hadn't yet moved the chest down to his bedroom. Perhaps it was pure exhaustion from the unusual amount of manual labor. Maybe he just didn't want the one thing in the attic that was of any particular interest to him to be removed from his sight while he worked. Either way, it sat there all the same.

At this point, you might be wondering why Jack hadn't bothered to look in that chest since his most recent experience in Ariel. The truth of the matter was that he was a bit scared of what might happen next. Everything Niko saw and experienced and felt could be seen and experienced and felt by Jack. He was living the life of a young man on the run from people who wanted to end his life. That wasn't a great thing to be a part of, even if the consequences might not catch up with him, and any more of it might leave him in worse condition than he was prepared to handle.

Jack was still a young boy, and though he had often dreamed of adventure, seeing what it was like in person was different than reading about it in a book or seeing it on television. He wasn't a superhero that could fight off all evildoers. He was a bit confused about who was the good guy in the first place. He had never thought it possible for an escaped convict to be a hero, yet he knew to his core that this was the case for Niko Monroe.

Jack glared at the treasure chest for the rest of his lunch break. Five minutes turned into ten and then fifteen. He took his last bite and decided he wasn't ready for more adventure. He'd rather scratch his way through the mess his grandpa had left him long before he had even been born. It was hard work, not to mention disgusting, but safe.

"I wonder what they're going to do with all this extra room in the attic," Jack pondered as he was getting to a point where newspapers were becoming less of a persistent pain. Other objects of little value and much scorn were giving him new problems and concerns in their place. It was becoming apparent his father was right about one thing...there wasn't much value in any of it.

Much like the suitcases he had worked on earlier, everything up in this attic was long out of fashion, if they were ever in some sort of style at any point in time. Worn, torn, and faded shreds of clothing, as well as shoes and blankets of all shapes and sizes, were scattered about without any more due diligence than the newspapers had been. His grandfather, it seemed, had treated the attic as a "maybe someday" room. This was the day, but it was Jack who was left to deal with the repercussions.

Maybe there had been a use in mind at the time, but Jack couldn't think of any reason to keep any of this old junk. There were no coin collections, no tools of any exceptional use, and not even a hint of a photo album or personal memorabilia. Just junk. No treasure.

The only thing that kept Jack going was that the pile of useless items was getting smaller and smaller by the hour. What he originally thought to be a great mountain, was turning into a very tiresome hill that needed some careful landscaping to become of some use to his family. He was determined to finish it as quickly as he could to enjoy the rest of his Christmas vacation. Perhaps it would snow again soon.

Still, something was gnawing at him. Jack wasn't sure what it was, but it felt like an itch that had not been scratched was spreading throughout his body, and he didn't know what would stop it. He just knew that there was something more to the attic than the piles upon piles of useless leftovers from a bygone era.

Jack tried to distract himself from the eerie feeling. He tried to come up with more games to pass the time. He soon realized that the effectiveness of his imagination was wearing thin. Newspaper basketball had come to an end and randomly scattered rolled up socks baseball wasn't as much fun. He tried to see if any of the old clothing scattered about could be donated to a thrift shop or a shelter, but they hadn't been well preserved in the slightest, years of dust and the hunger of moths had tattered them beyond salvage.

It did brighten his eyes, quite literally, when Jack managed to clear out enough of these undesirable items that he could finally open the one single window in the attic. It did take some muscle, and a few moments of grunting, but the window did swing out just in time for a gust of wind to blow inside and pelt the boy with a flurry of snow.

"Wait a minute," Jack said as he gathered himself. "It's not snowing outside. Where did that come from?"

It didn't take long for him to spot where the laughter had originated.

"Is that where you've been hiding the last few days?" said one of the Santos brothers.

"It's where I've been locked up!" Jack replied.

"Bad grades again?" said the other Santos brother.

"You guessed it!" Jack shouted. "Can't do anything fun until I clean out this whole attic. It's disgusting!"

"Well, if you ever make it out of there, it's supposed to snow again on Christmas!" the boy shouted. "Mom says you can come over whenever you want!"

"Thanks!" Jack shouted back. "But don't think I'll forget about that last snowball!" And he meant it. Best friends or not, Jack had a very long memory.

The two brothers ran off and Jack was left to his solitude. He was grateful for the minor distraction and happy for the fresh air. Nevertheless, nothing in the attic had found a purpose after all these years of storage. Seemed like such a waste.

Well, not nothing, he conceded. There was the treasure chest right in the middle. It wasn't glamorous, per se, and it didn't hold any gold or silver or anything like he had originally hoped, and what it did contain frightened him. He wasn't sure he wanted any part of it, though he couldn't take it off his mind, like an itch he couldn't scratch.

But that's the thing about itches. They don't go away just because you don't want any part of them. Sometimes they have to be scratched until they are no longer a nuisance or they burn. Jack was afraid it wouldn't go away so easily.

As the day drifted away, Jack felt a voice calling to him. It wasn't a shout, but more of a whisper in the wind, that beckoned him to open that treasure chest again.

"No!" Jack shouted. "I don't want any part of it. That's not my journey. That's not my life. That's not my problem!"

Jack crossed his arms and turned away. But a cold shoulder would not suffice this time. He had been summoned. He was called. He somehow knew he must open that treasure chest once again to face his fears. It didn't make any sense to him at the time, but it would come to him with the passage of events. He had to do this. This journey was a part of him.

Jack set down the garbage bag he had been filling and crept up to the treasure chest, slowly opened it, and with shaky hands picked up the map along with the pages he knew in his heart would continue the story. He closed his eyes, his sweaty palms begging him not to pursue the matter any further.

"I must do this," Jack assured himself, even as his body told him it would be better to choose flight over fight. "I have to know what happens next, even if I have to live it for myself. I need to see."

Jack took a deep breath, settled his shaking hands, and set his eyes on the pages before him.

Chapter Seven

A Clever Trick

The image burns deeper into my mind with every cycle on the television screen. My father's name appears below the ragged mugshot the State released to the government-funded news station. They didn't bother to clean him up before they took the picture like they normally would have with an ordinary criminal. They want everyone to see him like this, a wounded enemy with no hope for freedom. For the first time, they want the public to see how the State treats us, to see how citizens should treat an escapee if they ever happen to find one of us.

Six of us remain on the loose. Every one of us who made it out of the stadium has remained free, at least according to the reports, and I see no reason why they would keep such information from the public. The ones who remain in captivity are surely paying the consequences for our departure. The disparity between photographs of the two groups, those who are free and those who are not, is glaring. We are no longer a mere hunting trophy to our captors. We are a symbol of freedom that must be squashed.

My father may have taken the worst of it, but I believe he can handle it better than anyone, having led a life of selflessness and suffering, and I suppose that's what made him such a fearsome enemy to the State. I'm not sure his companions are faring so well under such conditions. They're older and weakened through days of mistreatment at Justice Hall. The beatings behind closed doors will only make them long to make their final sacrifice, the ultimate escape to freedom.

Those of us who fled the stadium have a different challenge set before us. The news reporter puts more focus on us than the others. Too much time spent on broken men and women will only lead to sympathy. But fear of those remaining in the shadows will override any time citizens might have to concern themselves over our brethren. They want the entire region to know our faces, names, and the threat we carry wherever we go. We are younger, stronger, and will have to survive on our own.

I'm thinking about more than survival every time my father's disfigured face appears on the screen. I see his disheveled gray hair covering a bruised eye. I see a slender figure the media wants to depict as miserable. His eyes betray their storyline. He must know I'm free. And I know I must help him join me.

"Do you have any more of these peanuts?" I ask my host.

"That was all of 'em," he tells me as he sets down an apple core on the table. "That was the last of our supplies. We must prepare to move tonight. This house won't be safe for much longer."

"Where will we go?" I inquire, trying to ignore the hunger which refuses to be silenced.

The old man stands up and walks over to a closet in the hallway. He opens a creaky wooden door and shuffles through a series of papers set in no particular order on the shelf before pulling out a single rolled-up sheet. He walks back toward the table where we had breakfast and lays out what I quickly recognize to be a map of Ariel City and its surrounding villages.

"We're in Evansville," he says, pointing to the tiny village on the eastern side of the map. The safe house is marked with a small circle in the center of the valley. There are none like it in any of the closest surrounding villages. "As you can plainly see, we have a journey ahead of us this evening, with few reasonable options. The house in Demascus was destroyed in a raid three months ago, so heading northwest from here would be a complete waste of our time. That leaves two sensible possibilities for us in the northern sector. Salem is closer, but more populous, and therefore more dangerous to navigate. Akiva will likely take us until dawn, but causes fewer worries if we can reach it before daylight. I know you are weakened from your confinement and escape, but I suggest we make the trek eastward to Akiva without delay."

"Salem," I say. "We have to go to Salem."

"Did you not hear what I just said?" he grunts. "Salem is stocked with guards and citizens willing to give us up for any amount of bounty. They'd turn us in for a day's pay."

"I know people in Salem," I tell him. "It's a callous town, full of hard-hearted men, but I know the guardian of its safe house. I know the village like it's my family. And the other escapees are more likely to have fled there as it is closer to the city than Akiva. We have to go to Salem."

"Nothing good has ever come from Salem," he says, furiously shaking his head. "If we go there, we're going to run into trouble. Safe house or no safe house, we will not be free of danger. I don't care who you know, we need to go to Akiva."

"You don't understand. My father built the safe house in Salem," I tell him. "If I say we're safe in Salem, then we're safe in Salem. I promise I can get us there without harm."

"Your father is a fool," he tells me, suddenly towering over me like a giant, his eyebrows furrowed and his fists clenched. "I told him to never go there in the first place. I told him he would be caught like a rabbit in the wild. Do you think you were captured in Alvaro for no reason? Guards from Salem followed you there, knowing you wouldn't have anyone to protect you. You think Salem is safe? It's a trap!"

"You knew my father?" I ask, trembling at his words, but I am cut off by a disturbing attack of white noise that sends me to the ground in fear.

"Get up. It's just the radio," he says, his gigantic frame now walking over to the machine next to the television screen. He grumbles as he gets down to one knee to adjust the frequency. "This might be important."

He knows my father. He knows me, or at least about me, but how? I stare at him as he twists tiny knobs on the transmitter. There is so much I'm sure he isn't telling me.

"Is someone out there?" he asks through a tiny microphone in his hand. "This is the Elder, can you hear me?" He taps at the device, attempting to get it to function properly.

The Elder. My father spoke of him on our travels, but he told me he had been captured, just as we eventually were, and had faced execution himself. Is this the legend or an impostor?

"I repeat, this is the Elder, do you hear me?" he says with urgent clarity.

"*Kreaacchhhhh*," a voice says over the radio. "*Gurg, kurf, serrrrsshhh.*"

"Blasted radio," he says, slapping his palm against the box. "This is the Elder, can you hear me? Are you in danger?"

"Yes," a voice says clearly. "My name is Rafe. Are you really the Elder?"

I know him. He's one of the twins. He's alive. The news reports are true. That means there are others. It means my father must still be alive or they would have reported his death. The State has an agenda, for sure, but the details must be correct or they will lose the trust of the people.

"I am," says the one who calls himself the Elder. I don't think he's lying.

"How can I know for sure?" Rafe asks, his voice muffled by white noise and someone barking orders in the background. "I heard you were in prison, maybe dead."

"Good," the Elder tells him. "That's what I had hoped was said of me throughout the State. Nevertheless, I am alive, and I am with… come over here, son. This is how you know I am telling the truth. Speak."

"Rafe," I say, bending my knee down to the ground to speak into the microphone. "It's Niko. Are you okay? Are there others with you? There should be six of us who made it out of the arena."

Silence.

"Rafe?" I ask again.

"Sorry, sorry," he says, leaving his radio on. I can't tell if he's laughing or crying on the other end. "We're all here. The other five of us are here. We're all alive."

"Where are you?" the Elder asks, taking the microphone back out of my hand, my task of confirming his identity having been completed.

"We're in Salem," he says. "At the safe house Niko's father built. There's food here, and bandages, blankets, everything we need for weeks. Enough to heal from everything they did to us in Justice Hall. Where are you?"

The Elder sighs. He stares at the screen that's now inches from his face. He sees the names of the captives and sinks his head into his free hand.

"We're in Evansville," the Elder reluctantly confesses. "We'll be headed your way this evening, just the two of us. We have run out of rations and need to move. You're not safe in Salem either, but you have supplies that we'll need before we proceed. Don't let anyone else in there unless they know the passcode."

"Passcode?" Rafe asks.

"Do you see a green bookshelf from where you are in the house?" the Elder asks, his voice steady, though his eyes are on fire.

"No," Rafe replies. He is silent for a moment, then cuts back in to say, "Wait…what's that over…yes, there it is, hidden in the corridor."

"Precisely," the Elder confirms. "You'll find a red book on the third shelf. It's the only one of its kind and looks like it doesn't belong. Inside you'll find a loose paper with instructions on how to greet us upon our arrival. Stay on guard. Stay off the radio. We'll reach you before dawn. Farewell."

The Elder turns off the radio, rips the microphone out of the wall, then makes his way to another room. Before I can ask him what he is doing, he returns with a strong wooden rod, which he feels against the palm of his hand before taking it to the radio, smashing it into small fragments that splash across the room. He takes one last look at the television screen and repeats in haste to destroy our only other method of hearing from the outside world.

When he completes his task, he looks at me like a lion, fierce and ready to move. "It's time to go," the Elder tells me. It's not a question.

"It's still light out," I remind him cautiously. "I thought we were waiting until dark."

"There's no time for that," the Elder says, offering me his hand. I take it and work my way back up to my feet, still sore from yesterday's journey. He storms over to a closet, where he pulls out a black long sleeve shirt with a hood on the back, which he promptly shoves into my chest. "Put this on. It's not much, but we don't have much of anything these days. You can't go running around like…that."

The Elder opens the trap door where I first entered the safe house. I follow his lead after he scales down the ladder with a small flashlight in hand. I see markings on the wall that I couldn't see last night, drawings depicting the secrets to avoiding traps along the way, hidden codes that only those in the know could interpret, only the Faithful would understand the symbols. I should have been more careful. I should have listened to my father.

"You didn't cover up the entryway?" he yells when we reach the other end. "How could you be so foolish? You're just like him, reckless."

"I was disoriented," I tell him." I was dehydrated. I was hungry."

"You were careless," the Elder growls. "It's a good thing we're leaving. Someone would have spotted this within days. Helicopters have been swirling since the quake. You could have gotten us killed. No wonder you were captured so easily. Broad daylight indeed."

I don't answer him. He's furious and overbearing, but he's right. Carelessness is what got us captured in the first place. If it weren't for the earthquake, I wouldn't have made it to today, so who am I to argue with him? He is, after all, the Elder is he not? My father always respected his wisdom. But one thing is bothering me as we hop up and climb over the back fence, my ribs screaming with every twist of my torso. We're forced to hike down a narrow path along a steep and rocky hillside that only the desperate would take to venture out of town.

The Elder said I was "just like *him*." He said I was reckless, most likely, as he considers my father to be reckless. The Elder was always spoken of so fondly by my father, yet this man does not appear to return the same affection. I want to understand the connection, but now is not the time to dig for more information on the matter, not out in the open where our lives are in danger.

The sun will not fall away from us for a couple of hours, but he said we have no time to waste. After discovering my blunder of leaving the secret door to the safe house open, we may have had even less time than he thought. But the back trail will only leave us vulnerable to the path itself, rather than armed officials, as we climb down this rocky hill before facing the task of hiking up the grassy ascent to Salem.

Every step I take is accompanied by my desire to find something to eat, or at least a running trail of water, but my hopes are consistently suppressed by dry dirt and rock exposed to the light of day. I need something to distract my mind from hunger and thirst.

"How do you know my father?" I ask after slowing down to maintain some distance in case my question is received with wrath. But he doesn't answer, nor does he stop or slow his pace, preferring to ignore me altogether. I resume walking and repeat my question. I will not let him deter me from knowing. I can't trust him if I don't know him or why he is so callous toward my father's actions.

This time he stops, takes a deep breath, then says, "It's a long story, son. One that I am sure will be addressed at the proper time. But now is not that time. We must continue our path and reach our destination as prescribed. We cannot risk the chance of someone spotting us in the light of day in Salem. We must come upon the town in the darkest hour and flee the following night. You and your father may have found a haven here over the years, but times have changed quickly since your capture. If only he had listened to me when he had the chance. If only he had…"

The Elder doesn't say another word for a long time. He doesn't stop to look at the sky, nor does he let his gaze wander around for food. This serves to tell me that he's been this way before, and there will be nothing pleasant along the way. I could have gotten us to Salem quicker if we could have taken the streets, but I understand that the wilderness is the safest place to be.

I follow the Elder without another word for a great length of time, staying ten paces behind him as a matter of caution, watching his feet to see where he steps, unwilling to risk injury from a lack of vigilance. My body has suffered enough damage. The sun creeps behind the hillside, leaving us a hint of light for a time before it is extinguished for the night. What little warmth we received from the sun disappears along with it and a cool breeze soon chills my neck as we reach a small lake.

"Water," I say, falling to my knees, dipping my hands in the cool lake before I'm jerked back by a tug on my shirt.

"Fool," he tells me as I pick myself up off the ground. "Do you see that water running anywhere? You're going to get yourself killed acting like that. You can't drink pond water. It's nothing but mud and animal remnants in there. No wonder you were caught so easily."

The Elder wipes his forehead and begins the ascent toward Salem. The path winds around a corner, and there's no way to see the end of the trail, but I am sure the hike is still much longer than we have traveled so far. We return to our mutual silence as we continue, yet all

I can think about is how much he claims to know about me and my father. I don't understand his anger toward our captivity, as if it were our own doing, especially when I consider that he too was once a prisoner, according to my father.

The path leading to Salem is wet and steep, my legs shake with every step through the grass and mud. My feet dare the ground to catch them awkwardly and snag me down to the muck, but I dare not lose step with the Elder. He is surly and agitated, but I wouldn't be able to make this trip without him. I've never gone on such a mission alone.

I've always walked side-by-side with my father on these trips, often with others in our company, consistently treated with care along the way. This man may care for my safety, but he does not suffer my negligence. If I'm ever going to receive answers from him, I'm going to have to offer him more than a sad story or a pitiful eye. He needs to know I can be of some use to him if he is ever going to trust me.

Without a street light in sight, the man I only know as the Elder stops in his tracks. It's so dark out here that I would have walked right into him if I hadn't been tracing his steps along the way. But his vision must be stronger than mine because he sees something that makes his muscles tense and his hands form back into fists. It takes me a moment as I scour into the distance with only a hint of moonlight escaping the cloudy skyline, but when I see it I remember why I never liked these back roads.

"Don't move," he whispers. "That's a…full grown…"

"I know what it is," I tell him, looking at our surroundings before making any further judgments. "I think it's alone."

I take a step forward.

"I said don't move," he whispers harshly.

I ignore him. I stare into the steely black eyes of the jaguar and make myself look as large as possible with my hands shaped into claws. The jaguar stays down low in its creeping position. I take another step forward.

"You fool," he rebukes me.

I hop forward and make the loudest, nastiest growl I can imagine. The cat remains unmoved. I stare him down and wait for him to indicate if he wants to attack me. I sneer, hiss, and stand my ground.

"You are going to get us killed," the Elder insists, but his mouth is shut when the jaguar makes his move. One paw moves forward. His tail flaps in the blustery air. He turns his head and jaunts up the hillside. "Well, I'll…"

"Apologize?" I say. "No need. But you might want to admit that you don't know everything about these hills. And you might want to tell me just what it is that makes you think me to be a fool or why you hate my father."

"You think I hate him?" he scoffs. "Your understanding is limited and your assumptions are hindered by lack of knowledge and wisdom. That was a clever trick to tame that beast, but you have much to learn about this world. We have to keep moving, lest he returns with a few of his friends."

The Elder brushes my shoulder and continues the climb toward Salem. His answers are vague and confusing, but we have little choice but to trust each other at this point, at least until we find a better place to lay our heads at night. For some reason, despite his apparent age and moniker, his endurance dwarfs mine as he pushes his legs up the winding road with ease and grace while I lumber behind him, winded and out of recourse to convince him to slow down. After all, he wants to beat the sun to Salem. I pray we find the safe house to be a place to eat and sleep.

Whenever I think I can't take another step, images of my father's mug shot on the television screen enter my mind, and I know I have to continue, if not for my sake, then for his. As long as he has oxygen in his lungs, I'll believe there's hope for his rescue. God provided a way out for some of us, perhaps the rest may yet have another chance.

My eyes are glazing over, but if they do not deceive me, I believe I see the faint sparkle of town lights in the distance. Salem, though great in number, behaves like a smaller village, and therefore retains little respect from Ariel City beyond the attention needed to police them, yet those who have wandered into its gates understand their power.

When we reach the town, I see they have blocked off all nearby side entrances. I look at the Elder, and though he must be as disappointed as I am, he seems eager to walk toward the main gate of this walled-in village. Perhaps he is tired of running and wouldn't mind if we were caught. Maybe he knows the gatekeeper and how to bribe his way through security. Or, as I find out long before we reach the entryway, he knows of more clever ways to reach our destination.

"Why are we going this way?" I ask in a hushed voice, though my speech travels further than I would have liked. "I know how to get to the safe house and this isn't the way."

"Not the way you know, you mean. No more talk until we reach the safe house," he says. "You don't know how to whisper. Follow my lead and we'll be there momentarily."

Without further reproof, the Elder unearths a key from a bush that has grown up against the brick walls. He then leads me fifty paces beyond the bush, presses it into the ground, and has the cover removed in the blink of an eye. He hands me his flashlight and points me down into a dark chamber. He waits until I reach the bottom, looks around for guards, then follows my lead, not failing to replace the grass-laden cover behind him.

I wait for him to reach the ground before I flick the light around the room, but I see no such markings as the ones back in Evansville. This is something different. This is something only he knew about. He's been here recently. The Elder snatches the flashlight back out of my hand and proceeds down the damp hallway. He couldn't have made such a maze by himself, so he must have discovered it, and he must understand he wouldn't be found if he used these tunnels.

"It isn't much further," he says, flashing his light up and down, looking for our opening while maintaining sure footing. "Ah, there it is. Stay quiet when you exit. We are by no means in the clear."

I follow him up the ladder and through the cover to see that day is now breaking. We are out of time. We must locate the safe house, and I'm not sure if this is a good thing or not, but we're in the heart of the village. Someone might have seen us climb up through the manhole on Main Street, but we won't give them time to find out why we're here.

Salem is populous for a village, but not large in area, which I think is what has been keeping it from ever gaining recognition as a true city. People are packed in tight with buildings that often rise four to five stories, including the one we are looking to find ourselves. I've been here many times, but it's been a long while, and the streets are too similar to easily differentiate one from the other. But I'm certain the Elder has been here recently too, and leads the way, darting in and out of alleyways to the only place in the town where we might find peace.

He knocks twice on the door. No one answers. Good. If anyone had begun to unlock the front door, we would have known to run. The most obvious entryway is never the answer. We walk around to the back of the house and he knocks three more times. We wait. He knocks three more times. We hear a faint knock from the other side. He knocks once more and a hatch opens to our side. We climb through and walk up the stairs to meet our hosts.

"Finally," a young woman says from her perch in the corner. "We don't have much time. Help us with the rations so we can go on our way."

Chapter Eight

No Other Choice

"How long do we have?" I ask, rubbing my eyes.

"Ten, maybe twelve hours, Niko," the Elder tells me as he offers me his hand. "Now get up. Tonight's journey won't be any easier than the last."

Two hours was all they gave me. I could have slept for twenty-four. I stretch out my back, wiggle the soreness from my body, and roll over to push myself up from the tiled floor. When I make it to my feet, I see a blurry image of a young man whose voice I recognize before my eyes see him distinctly.

"Follow me. I have to show you something," says Wiley, Rafe's twin brother. "Come on, it's in the lab."

"Lab?" I ask, but he ignores me, leading me through the narrow hallway to one of the back rooms. When I arrive, I see bunks converted into desks, laptop computers turned into a sophisticated network of machines depicting an array of maps, with a radio running quietly in the corner. "What is all this?"

"Isn't it great?" Rafe asks. He's sitting down in a disheveled black swivel chair as he manipulates the screens to show me the hub's capabilities. "Whoever was here last, knew what they were doing. They left everything I needed to set this all up. I've laid out our best course of action on the center screen. The trip to The Port won't be short, but it will be safer if we take the byways through the hills."

"Wait, The Port?" I ask. "Who decided we're going to The Port? You're just asking to be arrested. We need to go to Akiva."

"No," Rafe says, shaking his head to the point where his whole body wobbles. "Not Akiva, we have to go to The Port. Akiva is a death sentence. Look at this map I unearthed from the State's computer network. The red dots represent the State's armed guards from town to town. The larger the dot, the more presence they have in a certain village. Look for yourself, Akiva has more guards than any other town per capita. We might as well hand ourselves in. We're going to The Port."

"I have to show this to the Elder," I tell him.

"You don't have to show me anything," he says, hovering over us. "I've seen the schematics, the numbers, and the layouts. They're lying to you."

"I found these on the State's own network," Rafe insists.

"I know," the Elder says. "And how hard was it for you to uncover this information?"

"Not very. I'm good at what I do," Rafe says.

"I'm sure you are, but the State is smarter than you think. You found what you were looking for and moved on, just like they wanted you to do. But those aren't the real plans, and The Port isn't as safe as that map tells you it is. Tell me, which village do you think the State would want to protect? Some rinky-dink town like Akiva, filled with people who make their living from growing vegetables, or The Port, the region's major transit center? We're going to Akiva. We'll be safe there long enough to prepare."

"Prepare for what?" I ask.

"What's this I hear about Akiva?" asks a young woman entering the room. She's the same one that greeted us when we entered the safe house, if you can call it that. "I thought we were going to The Port."

"Change of plans," says the Elder. "Right, Rafe?"

Rafe looks back at his computer, twitching as he relinquishes the thought that he had figured out the State's weaknesses so easily, before turning and nodding his head a single time.

"Sheffield, Felicity, get in here!" she yells. "These guys say they want to go to Akiva now."

"Akiva?" asks a muscular man entering the room, who looks like he must be a year or two older than me. He's followed by a young girl, the one who fell at the Vespasian. I know little about Sheffield, but he carries himself like he's the leader of the other escapees. "Have you lost your mind? Didn't you show him the maps you found, Rafe?"

"The Elder says the maps are fake," Rafe tells them. "He says we're safer going to Akiva because it's not an important village to the State."

"Of course it's important to the State," Sheffield scoffs, throwing his hands up in the air. "They have a huge base on the west side of the village. I saw guards go in and out of there every day when I was a kid."

"You're from Akiva?" I ask.

"Lived there my entire life," he says. "At least until my time in Justice Hall. I lived two blocks from the base until I was arrested on some trumped-up charges. I didn't deserve to be in that hell and I'm not going back. Akiva is every bit as dangerous as that map shows."

"It's a lie," the Elder presses. "I believe you when you say there were military trucks entering and exiting every day, but they weren't filled with guards. There's nothing to protect in Akiva. It's a storage facility, not for weapons, but for food supplies in case of an emergency."

"An earthquake just happened the other day," says the young woman who has yet to introduce herself properly. "Won't they constantly be taking supplies into Ariel City right now?"

"Not that sort of emergency," the Elder shakes his head. "Enough of this conversation. We don't have time to argue. We have to get ready to move."

"Who put you in charge?" Sheffield retorts.

"Let me make this clear for you, kid," the Elder says, moving in close to the chiseled young man, undaunted by Sheffield's muscle-bound frame. "I'm not going to waste my time arguing with someone with limited information. We are all in grave danger and we have to find the safest place for us to go. I know this region, I know these towns, and I know the system inside and out. If you want to die with your companions, then please lead the rest of these youngsters into the busiest village surrounding the capital of the most powerful nation left in the world. But if you want to survive, if you want to make it year after year as the outcast that you now are, just as I have since you were a schoolboy, then you will take my directions as I give them. Got it?"

Sheffield looks over to the others, who are too busy staring at the floor to signal their consent. I can see his mind pacing back and forth, looking for an alternative, something that won't destroy what he had so quickly built up in his mind.

"We need to stick together," I tell them. "And we have to be united. A house divided will fall. I don't know about all of you, but I don't plan on falling, and the Elder's reputation should be enough for us to trust him."

I look to Sheffield, whose breath is in his nostrils, his fists clenched under his armpits, and his eyes scouring the room for any sign of dissent.

"What do you think, Maia?" Sheffield asks, looking over to the one who had greeted us upon our arrival. So that's her name.

Maia scrunches her nose, her eyes half-hidden by strands of brown hair covering her face, quickly sizing the Elder up and down. "I've heard enough," she says with a crisp voice. "We've made it through a rough couple of days, and we've proven we can survive through harsh times, but that doesn't mean we know enough about these villages. Most of us spent our lives secluded in different towns surrounding the City. We can't know as much about the region as someone who has spent years dodging the State. If we're going to trust someone, it might as well be him."

Sheffield spits on the ground. "Anyone else?" he asks, but the younger ones don't have the courage to choose sides, leaving him without support. He has lost the battle.

"So it's decided," the Elder says. "We head to Akiva at nightfall. Come on, it's time to gather provisions for our trip." He heads out of the room, shouting orders, as the others begin to follow him without further delay.

I'm about to leave the room as ordered when I feel a tug on my shoulder. It's Sheffield.

"What's your deal?" he asks me, grasping my collar, his eyes fixed on mine. "You two come in here in the middle of the night and you act like you're in charge of us. So what makes you trust this guy so much? Is he your father or something?"

I grab his hand and swing it away from me. "He's not my father. He's the Elder and if you're one of the Faithful then you should know as well as the rest of us that his reputation precedes him. And he's the best chance any of us have of living to see another day."

"Stop it, Sheffield," Maia commands. "Quit acting like you're the alpha dog. You know as well as the rest of us that we need help if we're going to survive. You might look tough, but we need an expert, and whoever the Elder really is…he's what we've got."

"I don't care," Sheffield says. "I don't need any of you. I made it here all on my own, didn't I? I'm the only one in here who can say that. The rest of you had to pair up to find this place. I'm a survivor."

"The rest of us know we need each other," I tell him. "Feel free to go at it alone, if you will, but you're not going to like the results."

Maia stares at us, shakes her head, and blows the hair out of her eyes as she walks past us and out of the room. Sheffield brushes his shoulder against mine and pushes his way into the common area where the Elder is laying out his plans. I take a deep breath and walk into the room in mid-sentence.

"Nice of you to join us, Niko," the Elder says, interrupting himself, before asking Rafe to retrieve one of the laptops. Rafe rushes to the other room as the Elder asks each of the others what skills they possess.

Everyone already knows what Rafe has to offer, but the one I always thought to be the crazy twin has his own abilities, though somewhat less sophisticated. "I like to blow things up," Wiley says with a twisted smile. "Back home I was known for my collection of dynamite and grenades as much as I was for anything else. If I hadn't been arrested for the faith, I probably would have found myself in prison for setting off an explosive in the wrong place or at the wrong time.

The Elder nods and looks over to Felicity, the youngest of us all, and waits for her to say something. She withdraws her eyes from his gaze as she thinks about what she can offer the group. "I'm...small," she says meekly, her voice audible, but lacking confidence. "And sneaky. I don't know what else I have to offer, but I'm good at hiding. I was the last one in my village to get caught for being one of...you know...one of us. I could have made it longer, but I was running out of food. I don't need much, but..."

"Very good," the Elder says. "And what about you?" he asks Sheffield. "How can you help?"

Sheffield puffs out his chest. "I'm strong," he boasts. "I can carry the supplies. Put it all on my back and we'll be fine. It's not like any of these other ones have any meat on them."

"Too risky. They will all have to learn to carry their own load," the Elder says. "But I'm sure we can find something useful out of your strength. Who's left?"

"What about your boy?" Sheffield asks. "What does he have to offer?"

"I told you, he's not my father," I reply, trying to control my temper.

"I know the trails," Maia cuts me off. "I've been in and out of the villages since I was a little girl. I may not know which towns are safe anymore, maybe I never knew as much as I thought I did, but if we need to get to a town, then I know the shortest route. I can get us to Akiva in half the time you have planned for us."

"About time one of you said something pertinent," the Elder grunts as he grabs the laptop from Rafe, sets it down on the table, and quickly manipulates the screen. "Please, my dear, show me on this map the way you intend to take us."

"The trails I know are not on any map," she says with a mischievous smile. "And we won't be taking the beaten path to get there. I know some of us have been more weakened by Justice Hall than others, but we don't have the luxury of staying in plain sight. We can begin by hiking up these hills, cutting through this side of the forest, and skipping over the narrow points of several creeks, but we won't be found by guards out there."

The Elder smirks and looks around at the rest of us. He proceeds to explain everything we will need to make it to Akiva. His plan is to stay there, if at all possible, until the State believes we are a lost cause. That won't be easy. Everyone knows our names. They'll recognize our faces. We're eventually going to need a better plan, and he knows that, but we have to get there first.

One answer the Elder did not receive, of course, is what I have to offer the team. If I was pressed any further, I'm not sure I would have an answer to give them. I'm not an expert on anything like the twins are with technology and explosives, nor physically gifted like Sheffield, and I'm not sneaky like Felicity. I thought I knew the trails well enough, but Maia's knowledge far exceeds my own in this region. But I'm as resilient as the rest of them and we're all in this together. I hope I find a way to prove myself.

Maia grabs me by the arm, turns me around, and stuffs a backpack into my stomach. "Snap out of it," she tells me. "I don't know what's going in your head, but there's no time for delay, we've got to get these filled and ready to go by sunset."

I nod my head and try to remember the Elder's instructions. We need supplies that will help us in every situation, not just food, but tools and communication devices. We all expect regular people to forget about us in time, but president Shah won't rest until our necks are broken, with or without cameras recording the action.

I head to the back rooms to see if I can help Rafe with his

equipment, but when I arrive it's the Elder sitting at the command station, listening to the State's radio news station. I dare not bother him, but I have to know what's going on for myself, so I stand silently and listen.

At first, it's the same rhetoric about our dangerous natures and information on what to do if we are sighted on the streets of Ariel City or in any of the villages. The lies don't phase me like they once did. It only takes two or three thousand conversations with patriots to realize they'll believe anything the State tells them to believe. They don't want to bite the hand that feeds them. They don't know what it's like to be the one who is bitten.

They repeat the names of those of us who have escaped, expressing their deep concern for the safety of those living in the villages, and the assumption that we are alive until proven dead or captured. Everything they have said has surely been regurgitated a thousand times since the day we fled and will continue until they receive a breaking report.

"We have new information regarding the six escaped convicts," says the surly male voice. "Authorities believe they are in the company of notorious outlaw Bramm Coyle, who is infamous for his role in the last known prison break a decade ago. Coyle, impersonating a prison guard, was involved in a plot leading to the escape of five men and women from Justice Hall, three of whom were never found, and one who was set to be executed on Independence Day before the earthquake struck. There have been no sightings of the reclusive con artist in well over a decade. We will provide more information as the

State gathers intelligence on the matter."

The Elder turns off the transmission, clasps his hands together, and stares at the monitor. I know better than to say anything, but Rafe comes in the room and starts packing his equipment into his pack. The Elder ignores him for a minute or two, but eventually gathers the strength to push himself out of the chair, walks around me without looking me in the eyes, and heads out.

I'll talk to him about this, but this is not the time. I look over to Rafe and ask if he needs help with his equipment. He blinks his eyes repeatedly while shaking his head. "Too important," he tells me. "I can't let any of this stuff out of my sight. I'll let you know if there's anything extra you can carry when I'm done here."

I shrug my shoulders and leave the room. I look for the next best place to start jamming my pack full of supplies when I bump into Maia in the hallway.

"Your pack is still empty?" she asks. "Do you think this is a joke?"

"I was attending to another matter," I tell her, unwilling to get into a debate at the moment, moving on without another word.

"Don't prove Sheffield right," she says before I turn the corner and enter the kitchen.

I don't acknowledge her statement in any way, but I know what she means, and I agree. I have to prove myself, not to him, or anyone else, but to myself that I can be of some value to this group. Before my capture, it was enough that I was the son of Hobbes Monroe. No one questioned his authority among the Faithful. He was bold in speech and convincing with wisdom. I was supposed to be just like him, but I was always in his shadow and never made it out with my own identity. Never thought I'd be in this position.

I start to sort through shelves and cabinets, looking for anything that could be of use to the group. The food supplies are all chosen to last for as long as possible, but some are more portable than others. But I'm less concerned with the food, which the others have mostly ravaged already anyway, and more concerned with tools. I search for knives and anything that could be used as a stake or hammer. My pack is half full when Rafe runs around the corner, grabs me by the shoulder, and tells me he changed his mind.

"I can't get it all," Rafe explains. "There's too much for a little guy like me. How much room do you have left in your pack? Looks like plenty. Come on."

I follow him back to the room, this time having made some progress to satisfy the others in holding my own, but no one is around to see it. I haven't heard much chatter from anyone since we broke apart for preparations. Everyone except Sheffield has acknowledged that we need each other to outlast the State's pursuit. They'll never stop pursuing those they consider unstable and threatening criminals, but none of us truly know each other, except for the twins.

Sure, I spent some time with Rafe and Wiley in the cafeteria, but even then we were too focused on our bread, soup, and impending execution for much dialogue. I know little of the others, and I doubt they know each other very well either. Then there's the Elder, who my father knew in the old days, but maintains a shroud of mystery around his speech.

I watch Rafe as he busies himself packing my bag with what looks to be the heavier items from his console. He repeatedly tells me to be careful with nearly every item, explaining their importance and function in the process, not that I understand anything he tells me. I nod my head as I think about how to maintain their safety through whatever hidden path Maia has planned for us. "Don't fall. Got it."

"Are you fellas about done?" the Elder asks softly after quietly entering the room. His typical audacious demeanor must have been tempered by what he heard on the radio, though I can see in his hand that his wits have kept him moving forward with a full pack, pockets stuffed on every side.

"Almost," Rafe tells him as he jams a keyboard into my pack. I regret offering him my assistance. I hardly had the chance to put anything in there that would be of any use to us on our journey, let alone to myself if for any reason I am separated from the others.

"Can I talk to you?" I ask the Elder.

"No," he says. "There's no time. The sun will set soon and we must be on our way."

"You can't keep secrets from us," I tell him. "You need to explain what the news reporter was saying. Who is Bramm Coyle?"

"Bramm Coyle is a figment of their imagination," he answers briskly. "And a useful one to our cause as well as theirs. The State doesn't want people to know about me, so they conjured a story about the day I escaped with a few other captives. There was never a Bramm Coyle in the employ of Justice Hall. Only an old man with more understanding than they liked. Now get your gear. It's time to go."

His answer was every bit as gruff as I expected, but if he thinks I'm going to let him slide away like that without further explanation then he is mistaken. If the State has the people thinking Bramm Coyle is with us, real or imagined, it means officials know the Elder is the one who has really joined our cause.

Rafe hands me back the pack, and just as I feared, it's a heavy load. I lug it over one shoulder, then shift the weight to the center as I wrap my other arm through a strap. The Elder leads us back to the main room where the rest have already gathered. The others have packs just as full as mine, but with varying weights and supplies. Their eyes look as tired as mine feel. Everyone has suffered more than any man or woman should in a lifetime. Yet we press on because we have no other choice. Seven rebels joined by a love for the Faithful and fear of the State. Seven individuals who must learn to act as one. We have a long way to go.

For a time, no one speaks, most of us more interested in catching our breath before we begin the long hike through whatever the forest has to offer us. If the skies are clear, the moon should provide sufficient light for our travels, but the woods are never without danger.

Then the Elder speaks. "I need to tell you all something before we go," he declares, looking directly at me before scanning the room again. "There are many things you do not know about me or my past. I understand that rumors swirl when it comes to my name and stature, and most of them are true, though often exaggerated or misunderstood. I will reveal everything in due time, but who I am and what I have done is of little importance to discuss right now. What matters is what I have seen and heard more often in my life than any man ever should. I have risked it all and lost more friends than I can count. I will not let that happen to any of you, not if you listen to me and heed my counsel. There are ways to stay alive and ways to die. The most important thing you need to know is that we are not dependent on our own abilities alone, but on the object of our mutual faith. We will make it to Akiva by the break of dawn, of that I can assure you, though danger lurks behind every tree along the way. It is now time for us to take our leave."

One by one we follow the Elder out through the hatch from which we first entered. The sun has hidden itself beyond the horizon and darkness surrounds us on all sides. It's going to be a long night ahead of us, but the streets are quiet and the path to freedom awaits. Maia walks alongside the Elder until we reach the edge of town. The rest of us follow in a staggered line. This is our life now. We will always be on the run. We have no other choice.

Chapter Nine

All That Fun Stuff

"Are they serious?" Jack said angrily as he regained his faculties. "They still haven't even worked out a real plan? They don't know what's out there! They're gonna get caught. I don't think I like how this is going to end."

Jack stomped back and forth in the attic as he tried to gather his thoughts. It was absurd. "Niko had been living on the road all that time with his father and still didn't know what to do next? He had to go get him, he just had to! How could he not have a better plan in mind?"

"What are you going on about?" Joshua Monroe asked as he climbed the steps to check on his son's progress. "Are you getting a little stir crazy or what? Looks like you've been putting in some work. Good, good. Another couple of days of hard work ought to do it, don't you think? You might just get to have some Christmas after all."

"You think?" Jack snarled.

"Lay off the attitude," his father shot back. "Your punishment is exactly what you need to get your thoughts on the right things. Besides, if you want to go downstairs to finish off those cookies your mother made for you, then you better not trip over your words on the way."

"Cookies?" Jack had forgotten all about the Christmas cookies he had made with his brother and sisters. His father barely had time to step aside as the boy jumped down through the hole in the attic floor and hopped downstairs toward the kitchen with a spring in his step that he hadn't been able to unwind for days. "Where are they?"

"On the counter, dear," his mother said. "Just where they always are. I told the others that they had to leave some for you, so don't be in such a hurry you forget to chew!"

Jack couldn't believe his eyes. After spending so many hours rotting away with the rest of the garbage up in the attic, he caught a whiff of the loveliest smell a boy his age could imagine. A sugar smorgasbord was set before him and he shoved two of the cookies in his mouth before bothering to look how they had turned out. It hardly mattered. They were always perfect.

"Is the attic clean yet?" Calvin asked as he looked in the fridge for a glass of milk to wash down his snack. "Mommy and daddy said you have been too busy to play with us all week."

"Way to rub it in," Jack said through the muffling of crumbs threatening to escape his jaw. "I bet you three have been running around doing all the best Christmas stuff without me."

"I thought you wanted to be up there," Calvin shrugged. "Mommy said it was a big deal for you. She said it was going to make you super-duper happy when you're all done. She said you get to…"

"That's enough, Calvin!" Mrs. Monroe said, quickly asserting herself into the conversation. "Jack is not going to miss out on any of the big Christmas traditions…that is…if he gets the attic cleaned in time."

Jack had a slight grin that nearly let crumbs fall from his face until his mother interrupted. "Wipe that smile off your face, Jack. You don't need to be giving your brother any guff about this either. Or your sisters for that matter. You're the oldest and with that comes certain responsibilities and privileges. You'll understand when the time comes."

Jack had no desire to be lectured. He finished chewing his cookies, grabbed a bottle of water, and headed back up the stairs, trying not to glare at his brother and sisters as they circled themselves around the dining room table to work on a jigsaw puzzle featuring three delightful snowmen in the woods.

When he got up the stairs and climbed his way into the attic, he saw his father sitting in a chair waiting for him. Jack didn't like the look on Joshua Monroe's face. Either he was in trouble or his workload was about to be magnified. His heart sank.

"What?" is all he could muster to ask as his father sat for a moment and stared.

"I just got a phone call from an old friend," Joshua Monroe told him, his voice as soft as the boy had ever heard. His beard had grown out a little extra over the first week of vacation, his perfectly combed hair had been recently ruffled by his sweaty palms, and his eyes had lost the sharp focus his son was accustomed to seeing. "I'm going to have to head out for a little bit. I'm not going to be able to help carry down the bags to the trash cans outside today like I was expecting. I know this has been a big task for you, but I'm going to need you to do a little bit more."

"But Dad," Jack tried to argue, his hands at his hips, a scowl overriding any memory of the sugar cookies, though a few crumbs remained on his shirt.

"Listen," Mr. Monroe said with little more than a whisper. "Sometimes life throws things at you that don't seem fair. Maybe you feel that way right now about cleaning the attic, but I need you to strengthen yourself and finish the job. That's all a part of growing up and becoming a man. Now I have to go and deal with something that I'm not very happy about and I need you to do all you can to get this room finished. You've done a great job so far, and I'm very proud of you for that, but your mission isn't complete."

Jack nodded his head and watched his father silently trail away to do whatever it was he couldn't bring himself to say aloud. He now had an empty feeling in the pit of his stomach, despite having just polished off several sugar cookies with hardly a breath between bites, and didn't feel much like wading through the rest of the huge piles of garbage.

Jack decided to open the window again to gather himself with some fresh air. He noticed the snow, which had gathered so bountifully on the first day of Christmas vacation, had receded to the point where patches of grass had begun to show themselves and roofs had hardly any icicles remaining.

"I missed my chance," Jack sighed. He knew it would snow again this winter, as flurries always came and went throughout the season, but one never knew if it would be days or weeks until the next good storm.

The streets were all but empty of people. Many of his neighbors, like Susie and her family, had simply gone away for a week or two. Others, like the Santos brothers, were surely at home enjoying hot cocoa and holiday movies with their moms and dads.

Jack, however, had been spending his days toiling away in a dusty attic with little compensation other than a set of terrifying visions that hardly made any sense to him. Why was this happening? Was it simply because he was the first to open the treasure chest in so many years or had it been waiting for him all this time as if it had been his purpose to find them? After all, whoever this Niko Monroe was, he had the same last name as Jack. That couldn't have been a coincidence, he thought, but what he saw hardly resembled any time or place he could recall seeing, even on television.

While he thought through these things, Jack began to muster enough energy to continue his work. He collected, examined, and tossed away piece after piece of garbage well into the evening.

Just like the other nights, Jack sighed with relief when dinnertime came and went and he was soon comfortably asleep in his bed. He had no dreams, no visions, no nightmares. Just sleep. And when he awoke, he had a clear mind and decided to make it a clean slate for another day of work in the attic.

"Today's the day," he decided to tell himself, his confidence at an all-time high. "I'm going to finish up that attic if it takes me until midnight. Then I never want to clean another thing in my life."

Jack made his way down for breakfast, where his mother had just begun to stir some orange juice for the four children. Calvin, Sadie, and Samantha had long been awake and had been quite anxious for the pancakes to be ready.

Eira Monroe, however, was lacking the usual pep in her step. Jack quickly picked up on what his siblings hadn't noticed.

"What's wrong, mom?" Jack asked.

"Nothing to concern yourself with," she told him.

"Where's dad?" he asked, not remembering any sign of him returning home the night before.

"He had to go see an old friend," she said with a sniffle she couldn't hide. "It's nothing I want you to concern yourself with right now."

Jack looked to his siblings and subtly shook his head while mouthing the word, "no." He knew it wasn't the right time for follow up questions and as the older brother he wanted to make sure they knew it too. He could sense something bad had happened, and it wasn't any of their business, but he would ask again later when the time was right.

The breakfast table was silent that day. The children ate what was on their plate and went their separate ways without so much as a moment of bickering or a selfish clamoring for this or that.

Jack knew he had better things to do than to waste his time

fighting over nothing when he could be upstairs polishing off the attic. Although it had been mostly junk he had been sorting, he still had hope there would be something that would help him understand the map along with the letters he had been finding in the treasure chest. There had to be an explanation for the visions, or whatever they were, that had let him see through the eyes of Niko Monroe.

Before Jack could round the corner up the stairs, his father walked into the living room, his jacket and face dripping wet.

"Raining outside today," Joshua Monroe said, his words flustered as he shook off his boots. "Better make sure that window is closed up there."

"Yes, sir," Jack said quietly, not sure if he wanted to look in his father's eyes at the moment. "Are you…never mind."

"It's okay, son," he said. "It was a rough night for my old friend. It's not something you need to hear about, but I think he's going to pull through."

Jack nodded his head and swiftly made his way up to the attic. His dad was talking through vague words, but was clear as day, and the boy knew he wasn't ready for such discussions.

Yet when Jack climbed back up to the attic, the first thing he looked at was the treasure chest, the one with the letters that had been showing him things all week, mysteries he knew he hadn't been ready to witness. It wasn't like television. He had seen things in movies that he knew he wasn't supposed to have seen, but they hardly affected him at all. Those weren't real. They came from someone's imagination. But the story of Niko Monroe was so vivid and the experience made too little sense.

"Maybe I should tell my dad," Jack contemplated to himself, not sure when his father might pop his head through the trap door again. "He might know what's happening. He always seems to be the one who knows what to do. People call him when they're in need. I've always called on him when I'm in trouble. But I don't know how I would even begin to explain this."

Jack went straight to work on the attic, busting his tail as he sorted through the diminishing piles of long faded items of clothing and miscellaneous junk his grandfather couldn't bring himself to throw away decades ago. But every minute or two Jack looked back at that treasure chest. It seemed less and less likely as the hours passed by that he would find anything resembling a clue, but he knew in his heart that those letters would keep coming if he continued to check for them.

The pile continued to evaporate before his eyes. Jack could hardly believe it. Christmas was right around the corner and he had nearly served out his sentence. He was so excited he started to become nervous. "What if this isn't all of it?" he wondered. "What if they have something more for me to do? They knew it couldn't take that long to clean one room, even if it had been treated like a wasteland."

When Mr. Monroe popped his head back up through the square in the floor, Jack looked at him with suspicion.

"Looks like you've just about wrapped it up here, have you?" asked Joshua Monroe with his eyes popped out in surprise. "I was hoping you would have some time left over."

"I knew it!" Jack yelped before he could cover his mouth. "I mean…you said this was my punishment, it's not fair to add any more work to it just because I did it fast. Besides I…"

"Hold on, Jack," his father said with his lip curling. "You know what, I almost let you get away with that right there. But why don't you go ahead and take the last couple bags of garbage downstairs and then I'll let you know."

Jack scowled. He scowled picking up the garbage bags, he scowled as he stomped down the stairway, and he scowled as he slushed his way through the pouring rain to sling the trash bags into the back of his father's pickup. Then he scowled his way back inside, scowled as he tossed his jacket on the floor, and scowled his way back up the steps.

He thought about not climbing his way back up to the attic. He considered running to his room and locking the door. But he knew it would be of no use. Somehow his entire Christmas vacation was going to be spent in this stupid attic.

And he was right. When he climbed up to the attic, he was surprised to see that it wasn't as empty as when he had left it. Joined by his father was his mother standing next to him with a nervous smile on her face. Next to them were Jack's three siblings, each jumping up and down on a mattress. His mattress.

"What is going on here?" Jack said with his mouth over his hands. "Why are they - how did that - what is happening?"

"It's your own roooooom," his brother and sisters giggled in unison as they continued to jump up and down on his bed.

"We wanted it to be a surprise," his mother told him.

"And we wanted you to learn what can happen when you put in the hard work," his father said pointedly. "And just because your punishment is over, doesn't mean you don't still have work to do. Everything you own needs to be brought up here before Christmas."

Jack had stopped listening. He knew what his father was saying and didn't need to hear it. His tired body suddenly felt light as air and he had springs in his feet. He wanted to jump up and down with his brother and sisters on his bed. Instead, he ran downstairs without another word to bring up some essentials for the first night in his new room.

He gathered his biggest flannel blanket, some matching sheets, a lamp, an alarm clock, and stuffed them all into the biggest duffle bag he could find. He skipped all the way back to the attic where he found his family had barely moved at all, except that his mother stood there with a broom and a dustpan.

"Did you seriously think we were going to let you sleep in here with all this dust lying around?" she asked him.

Jack stood there with a grimace. He hadn't had time to think much at all, let alone consider he would have to keep his room clean without any help. He had never really taken much care of his old room and it was obviously in much better condition than the attic.

"You have a little bit of time left until you need to sleep," his mother said as Jack's siblings began to tire from treating his bed like a trampoline. "Until then, you can take care of the cobwebs in the corners and the dust on the ground. Your father will help you with some of the more difficult tasks after Christmas, but you're responsible for making it livable for yourself. We expect big things out of you, mister."

Jack felt like a dozen heavy rocks had just been thrown inside of his duffel bag, but even when he dropped it to the floor, he felt no less of a burden. A punishment had turned into a surprise, which then turned into a change in perception regarding his role in the family. He was no longer just one of four siblings who happened to be the oldest. The boy was now going to be held accountable, as well as trusted with responsibilities. He was one step closer to manhood.

Calvin, Sadie, and Samantha were soon ushered off to their beds for the night. Jack wondered what Calvin was going to do with all the extra space in the room they had shared for so long, but the way his mother had been carrying herself gave him a clue. That was going to be a discussion for another day. He had enough on his plate as it was.

Jack took the broom from his father and began his work. He had no imaginary games left to play, no mysterious treasure hunts left to pursue within a mysterious pile of what turned out to be wall-to-wall garbage, and no endless tasks to complain about. He was left with sweeping, one of the most simple and uninteresting chores imaginable. It wasn't terrible. It wasn't fun. It was just something he had to do.

But Jack still had something else on his mind. He had tried to block it out. He wanted to push it out of his mind forever. He knew that was never going to be the case. He was going to have to complete the journey with Niko Monroe. He was going to have to finish the adventure. But it wasn't going to be this night.

Instead, Jack dropped his broom, the room half clean at best, and nearly collapsed into the bed that his mother had been kind enough to prepare for him with the items he had retrieved from his old room.

It was dark. The moon was hardly a sliver in the night sky and the clouds were blocking most of the stars. It hardly concerned him. The inside of his eyelids was all he wanted to see as he quickly dozed off for the night.

When Jack awoke the next morning, he had no desire to open his eyes. Christmas was two days away and he had hardly had time to celebrate the season. While his brother and sisters played and decorated, he had been busy purging and tossing and scrubbing his way to a new room. While they were happily devouring Christmas candy and watching their favorite holiday movies, he had been witnessing the life of another person, one whose troubles were far worse than his own.

Jack blinked. He did so repeatedly until his eyes came into focus and he saw his father fiddling with something from his toolbox. Mr. Monroe was sitting on the one thing they had left up in the attic that had been there all those years, the treasure chest that had contained a map and certain letters regarding the troubling times of Niko Monroe.

"What are you doing in here?" Jack quickly questioned his father.

"We have things to do today," Joshua Monroe answered. "Tomorrow's Christmas Eve. Don't plan on doing any work on a holiday. Do you?"

"Didn't think I had much of a choice," Jack answered honestly. "What are we going to do today?"

"Was it a bit cold in here last night?" his father asked, gesturing all around to the four walls of the attic. "Thought we might check on the insulation. Make sure the wiring up here is safe while we're at it. All that fun stuff."

"I don't know how to do any of that," Jack said as he climbed out of bed.

"That's true," his father nodded. "That's why you have me. I'm going to show you how to do those things so when you grow up you'll be able to show your son how to do them. That's how families work. You pass down what you know."

"So you learned all of this from grandpa?" Jack asked.

"I learned many things from my old man," Mr. Monroe said. "But he wasn't much of a handyman. Picked most of this up on my own. Your gramps has always been more of a philosopher, I guess you could say. A real thinker. He is more concerned with the meaning of things than some of the practical aspects of life. Guess that's why he didn't know what to do with all that stuff you just cleared out. He hoped to go out on a missionary journey someday. He was a faithful man, went to church every Sunday, but his dreams never materialized the way he hoped. Too busy raising a bunch of rowdy boys."

"A missionary journey?" Jack asked. "Like the people who go to other countries?"

"Just like them," Mr. Monroe said. "We come from a long line of them, you ought to know. Guess it stopped with grandpa. And my brothers and I…well…I suppose we were more needed around here."

Joshua Monroe spent that day doing all the things he could to help

Jack make his new room suitable for living. More work would need to be completed after Christmas, but he would be able to get through a few days of sleeping in the attic as it stood.

Throughout the day, Jack's eyes would wander their way toward the treasure chest, as he contemplated the contents of the box. Who was Niko Monroe? His father had never mentioned that name and he couldn't remember seeing it when he had scanned the old family tree for a school project. And the places. He'd never heard of them! It was a mystery, but one he didn't want his father knowing too much about. Not yet. He knew he had to find the answer for himself.

After dinner came and went, Jack went up to his room alone, sat on the floor in front of the treasure chest with his legs crossed and his heart beating rapidly. He was shaking, but confident in his decision, he had to see what was to become of Niko Monroe.

Jack opened the chest. He saw a now tattered map, realized he could recognize some of the names listed, and he knew where Niko was set to go next. With it was a hefty stack of crumpled papers leading him to believe it wouldn't be easy. He took a deep breath, settled in for the long road ahead, and opened his eyes as he continued the great escape.

Chapter Ten

The Great Escape

Security presence outside the village gates is limited. Guards won't chase us amongst the trees, but our steps are no less cautious. We follow Maia in single file through the dense forest, not knowing her path, and uncertain what awaits us in Akiva. The Elder claims it will be safe in such a small village. Sheffield thinks the old man is a fool. I know where I stand, but I don't know these people well enough to be confident in anything they say. We come from varying backgrounds, but the enemy has forced us to work together, and so we march on despite our differences, hoping our faith will secure our bond.

"We need to get to Akiva before sunrise," the Elder reminds Maia.

"That won't be a problem," she assures him.

Every step I take is a burden, the pain still shooting through my body from the day we escaped. This is the third day in a row I've had to hike to a new village. I thought with enough motivation I would be able to adapt to the rigors of the life of an escaped convict, but my time in Justice Hall left too little meat on my bones, and adrenaline wore off long ago. I don't know how much more of this my body can take. If Akiva doesn't provide the safety the Elder all but promised us, I might not make it to another safe house. No one is talking much, but when they do their tone betrays them. We're all suffering.

I feel relief whenever it looks like we're about to descend into a valley, silently praying we are approaching Akiva, but there's always another hill to climb, stream to sneak over, or series of swaying trees to dodge in the windy night air. If I've learned anything tonight, it's that if we ever find a place to rest, I'm going to need to prepare my body for a more treacherous life on the run. If this is how it's going to be from now on, I need to prepare my soul for what lies ahead or I'll end up dead, whether the State finds me or not.

"I recognize these rocks," Maia tell us, kicking a layer of small pebbles in front of her. "We're not far from the outskirts of the village now."

"How are you doing with my gear?" Rafe asks me.

"Don't worry about it," I tell him. "I know how to protect a pack."

"Okay, okay," he calms himself. "I'm just…have you ever been to Akiva?"

"Once," I tell him. "When I was young and I honestly don't remember it well. My father always spoke fondly of the town, but he never gave many details on why he thought so highly of the little village itself. I believe the Faithful in Akiva were few but strong. What the Elder said about farmland sounded familiar, but nothing else of significance comes to mind. How about you?"

"No," Rafe replies. "Our parents never let us go anywhere, really. Our trip to Justice Hall was the first time we left our home for more than a day or two. They never wanted us to get into any trouble with the law. It seems to have found us anyway."

"What's it really like, Sheffield?" Wiley asks.

"Why don't you ask the old man?" Sheffield answers sharply. "He seems to think he knows more about my own hometown than I do."

"There's a reason for that," the Elder barks, unconcerned about anyone hearing us until the village is in sight. "Not that you know how to shut your mouth long enough to figure it out, Sheffield. But it doesn't matter right now. We're not going to Akiva to see the town and chat up the locals. We are there to hide and prepare for the mission ahead of us. We won't be able to take the next step without proper attention to detail."

"The next step?" Maia asks, coming to a halt at the sight of street lights glowing down in the valley below us. "Since when are we on any mission besides survival?"

"Do you think we can run and hide forever?" the Elder asks us as he surveys the wall surrounding the village. "We are running out of safe houses in the region and they'll all be low on rations by now. The Faithful have dwindled, if by force or by fear. This might be our last chance of turning the tide."

"Turning the tide?" I ask. "The tide of what?"

"The State wants you to think it's strong," the Elder answers as he begins picking out different guard locations and points of entry, taking notes on a small pad he managed to carry in his pack. "Ariel is more fragile than they want you to believe. Their walls are cracking and their leadership is fractured. This is our chance to change everything."

"Didn't seem that way on Independence Day," Sheffield scoffed. "Looked like they all wanted our blood. Every one of them from President Shah to those animals in the stadium who cheered on our impending execution."

"Of course they did," the Elder frowned. "They're hanging on by the slimmest of hopes that the State is telling them the truth. Shah believes he can silence the dissenters with the slaughter of the Faithful. But your escape will have caused a murmur that even the president won't be able to contain with his iron fist and armed guards."

"So what does that have to do with us?" Maia began to ask, but she was quickly interrupted by the sudden jolt of the Elder's head. "Why are you ducking?"

The Elder didn't answer for five minutes as he put his hand over his mouth. The rest of us followed his lead, but it took me a minute to see what had caused him to hide. We soon witness two guards passing by no more than fifty feet in front of us. No one moves a muscle until they are out of sight and hearing distance.

"There's no more time for further explanation," the Elder insisted. "We'll get to that when we're in the safe house. I know of a way inside the walls over on the left side of that gate with the metal bars. The guards never pay much mind over there because that gate is rarely opened."

"Then what are we waiting for?" I ask, suggesting we go forward.

"You're not going to like it," the Elder answers. "It's through the underground tunnels hidden by that post over there, three hundred yards beyond the front gate, the one with the flag of Ariel on top."

"And by underground tunnels you mean…" Rafe sighed.

"The sewers," I sighed, my frustration coming through instead of anger. I'm so tired.

"I said you weren't going to like it," the Elder grumbles, spitting on the ground as he begins to lead us through the brush that quickly reveals a hidden layer of pavement, an unsuspicious entryway to those unaware of its presence.

"How do we open it?" Maia asks, the rest of us looking to the Elder for an answer.

"There's going to be a coded lock by the entrance," the Elder answers, pointing his now shaking hand toward a small manhole covered with fake sod and grass. I'm not the only one low on energy. No one is at full strength. "We're going to need to pick that lock to enter."

"Do we guess until we find the right code?" I ask, speaking before I realize I'm not the one who should be talking at the moment.

"Can't do that," Rafe shakes his head. "A coded lock such as this is likely to trigger an alarm if we were to guess wrong two or three times. Not a big deal if we were supposed to be there, but we're not, and we'd be met by guards faster than an antelope in the sight of a hungry lion."

"So how do we steal the code?" Maia asks, looking over her shoulder to make sure no one is looking our way. "It's not like we can inquire at the front gate."

"Leave that to me," Rafe tells her. "Niko, I need something I stuffed into your pack that should do the trick." He steps behind me and quickly searches through the side pockets and retrieves a small electronic device.

"What's that?" the Elder asks, admitting that even he was unsure of how we were going to get past the lock. "I've seen many peculiar devices in my day, but that doesn't look familiar."

"That's because I invented it," Rafe says, a grin piercing his dirtied face. "Came up with the idea a few months before we were apprehended. The prototype looks a lot better than this, but I had limited time and resources at the first shelter we came to. Just give me a moment and pray this isn't too loud when I snap it into…there, that ought to do it."

"You're a genius," I tell him as the lock slips loose and I help him lift the manhole under the flag pole.

"Imagine if the State had known," Rafe says with a wink. "They would have had me programming these under threat of force. Then no one would have been able to pick them."

"Glad you're on our side," Maia says as she follows us.

"That's why I like to keep him around," Wiley jokes before the Elder motions for us to all be quiet.

"We're not out of the woods just because there aren't any trees down here," the Elder chastises us in a hushed tone. "Keep your mouths quiet and your ears open. There could be guards down here or even a technician who would be keen on reporting us to them. There's a quarter-mile maze we have to navigate before we get to the safe house. Do your best to keep up. We don't know how much time we'll have to…did you hear…quick! Hide!"

I dive and roll behind a pillar, slamming my head hard against the corner of a metal cylinder. It's not the first time I've hit my head on something so unforgiving, but there's no preparing for it, and it always hurts. My eyes blur for a moment, and I have to shut off the screams inside my head, but I am able to find my senses and make out how the others have been discreet enough to have evaded the set of guards making their rounds.

"I wouldn't worry about it," a tall, slender man says to his partner, a short, stocky woman nervously tapping her radio against the palm of her left hand. "The governor comes here twice a year to make a political speech to his voting base, which is everyone who knows what's good for them. He's not here to stir things up. Nothing exciting ever happens in Akiva. I don't know why they still feel the need to tighten security whenever he's in town."

"Nothing exciting we know about," she says as they turn the corner. I can faintly hear her theorize, "But I swear there's something going on around here beyond our pay grade. Maybe it has to do with those convicts who escaped the other…"

The Elder lifts his head and motions for us to be quick and silent. I don't think they'll be back around this way for a while, but these catacombs are not as vacant as we had hoped. We all realize this is no time to let our guard down.

"How far is it?" I ask the Elder as quietly as possible while we slither from shadow to shadow.

"Not far," he whispers back, his eyes focused and his body tightly slinking through the alleys of the sewer. "But we have to be extra careful around this next corner."

"Why's that?" Maia asks.

"I've never seen a time when there wasn't a guard or two across the way from where we're headed," the Elder tells us as he pokes his head around the corner. "And I see three of them right over there, huddled up around a radio."

"What do we do?" I ask. "We've come too far to turn around."

"Turn around?" he scoffs. "They'll never be more distracted than they are by that radio. Turning around would be more work than getting past those three. Someone will surely stumble across that open lock we left out there sooner or later. If we're lucky, they'll think some local punks were out having a laugh, but any guard with a vested interest in their career would remember there are still a half dozen convicts loose in the region. We just have to pray this safe house is still operating according to its purpose."

"What if it isn't?" Sheffield demands to know. "What if we're walking into a trap?"

"We have no other options," the Elder insists. "It's this or nothing. If you want to turn back now, that's fine, I won't hold it against you. But I'll bet you'll regret it when you're tossed back into that cell in Justice Hall. How long do you suppose it will take for them to find you a new noose?"

I gulp. None of us have the experience the Elder has in these matters. We haven't lived this life for long. Even if we had a better plan, we wouldn't know how to execute it on our own. Our lives are in his hands.

"So how do we get past them?" Maia asks as I take a peek around the corner. "They must be on high alert if so many of them are roaming the sewers, looking for something suspicious. They could be talking about us right now for all we know."

"Wiley," the Elder beckons gruffly. "What kind of...distractions do you have in that pack of yours? Anything useful?"

Wiley grins like a cat with a bird in its sights. "Probably. Depends, though. What kind do you need?"

"We need something big enough, and far away enough, to send all three of those guards running down that corridor beyond them," the Elder says. "And we need them out of our way long enough for us to all get through that hatch hidden over on the other side, the one twenty feet high up that ladder, without them hearing, seeing, and capturing us."

"I can do that, but I'm going to need some help," Wiley answers as he tosses off his pack and locates a black and yellow device slightly larger than the size of his hand.

"I'll help," I say, looking to be of some value to the group.

"No," Wiley says. "I've seen you plop along in the forest enough now. I need someone fast and quiet. I need her."

Felicity looks around before pointing a trembling finger to herself as she shakes her head. "I don't know anything about bombs," she says, her soft chipmunk voice looking for a way out of harm.

"You know how to be quiet," Wiley tells her. "You didn't make a noise when we were walking through the forest. I can't say that about anyone else here. You might not be the strongest person here, but you don't need big muscles to silently hold a wire for me while I set off this explosive."

"Which explosive?" the Elder asks Wiley before Felicity can respond to his request. Wiley needs her for this. We don't have time for arguments.

"This one will have them putting out a fire," Wiley assures us. "A fire which won't want to go out, no matter what they use on it. A fire that will give us enough time to get through that hatch undetected."

"Go," the Elder says to them. "We will wait."

Felicity is frozen, except for her delicate green eyes, which are rapidly going back and forth as they search for one of us to give her a way out.

"It's okay, Flick," Maia tells her, leaning in and putting her hand on Felicity's shoulder. "We've been through worse. We got out of that arena, didn't we? This is a simple job. We need you to do this."

Felicity takes a deep breath, nods her head, and follows Wiley into a darkened path. I can barely see them as they weave through a maze of crates which conceal them from the guards, who have been getting louder by the minute.

"Think they're suspecting we might be down here by now?" I ask the Elder.

"No," he says quick and to the point. "No. I've seen this before. They're arguing because they have nothing else to do with their time.

How often do you think a security issue comes up in the sewers? No, if they were onto us, they wouldn't be arguing, they'd be in pursuit."

"How long do you think it'll take Wiley to do the job?" Maia asks.

"Not long," Rafe answers. "He's been training for this his entire life. He might not even care if he gets caught tomorrow if it means he has the pleasure of demolishing something today. He lives for this."

As if on cue, a light explodes from around the corner.

"Wait," the Elder holds us back. "Let them get out of sight."

"Wiley!" Rafe muffles a shout into his hands. "That wasn't enough time!"

"Flick!" Maia gasps. "I shouldn't have…"

We were all thinking the same thing. That should have been on a timer. There's no way they could have made it over there, set up an explosion, and escaped in time.

"Now!" the Elder begins to pull us up with him to run to the hatch two hundred feet from where we were hiding. No sign of Wiley or Felicity. They should have been waiting for us closer to the hatch. They should have gotten there before us. This isn't good.

The Elder points to the hatch door and motions for me to twist the handle. "It's stuck," I say too soon. It was tight, but it moves after the third attempt. Sheffield jumps through first, followed by Maia, Rafe, and the Elder. I turn around and see the flames still going strong. Wiley was right. They haven't put it out so easily. I begin to climb up the ladder with my stomach feeling like it had been punched. I grab the latch, but a hand stops me.

"You weren't going to forget us, were you?" Wiley asks before

Felicity slides around him and follows me up and through the hatch. Wiley takes one last look over his shoulder, lets a smirk spread across his face, then seals us in.

"Is this it?" I ask as I behold a small metallic room with no furnishing and low light. "Is the safe house?"

"Not yet," the Elder tells us. "But we're close. No more guards in our path."

We follow him through a small trap door, then a narrow maze of white walls which look like they've never been touched by man or beast, lit only by the Elder's flashlight. Within five minutes, we're at another hatch, this time a ladder leading us straight up to the safe house.

The Elder opens the hatch door and has to bite his tongue before a foul word can escape his mouth. He slams his hand against the wall, shakes his head, and moves forward, muttering for a moment.

"What is it?" I shout from the bottom of the stairs. "Guards? Do we need to run?"

"Just get up here," the Elder shouts, trying to hide his anger, but failing miserably. "No guards. No anything. Someone else got here first and didn't leave us anything."

"Nothing?" Sheffield complains. "No rations, no change of clothes, no weapons?"

"That's what I said - no, wait a minute," the Elder says cutting himself off. "I remember now. Everyone get up here immediately. The side rooms of this safe house have a thousand little secret compartments. It was a safety measure Niko's father came up with years ago. Not many were installed when the State turned on us, but this was one of them."

"Should we be looking out for traps?" Wiley asks instinctively. I wouldn't have thought of it. The Elder shakes his head, then explains to us what to look for and how to find it.

My mind feels miles away from my body as I consider how little use I have been through this entire trip to Akiva. I'm nothing like my father. He should have been here, not me. I can't help these people and I'm not entirely sure the Elder wants to. I gather he would be better off doing this alone, but he must have enough of an allegiance to keep him from ditching us, even if he's been cut off from the Faithful all this time.

"Found something," Maia shouts first. I've been through at least a dozen drawers and have come up empty. Her nose shrinks and her lips contract. "Sardines. Yuck!"

"I'll take those," the Elder says as he snatches it out of her hands.

"Whatever floats your wagon," she tells him.

"You haven't been on the run nearly long enough," the Elder replies. "A month turns into a year faster than you realize. Sardines help your brain function right. You're young, but you still need your wits about you."

"Here's something," Rafe shouts.

"Dibs," Wiley says as he snags it from his brother. "This will come in handy."

"What is it?" I ask as everyone shifts their eyes back and forth between what Rafe had found and the next cabinet, trap door, or hidden compartment we can get our hands on.

"Something to make the sky really pretty for about three seconds," he answers. "Which might be the three seconds we need to get out of another tight jam."

"Keep looking," the Elder orders us. "Check every door. We need everything this place will afford us."

The safe house is larger than I imagined. I didn't know something this large existed within the Faithful's meager means. There must be two dozen rooms, each lit brightly from a generator I assume must be connected to solar panels above ground. No one among the Faithful could pay for the amount of electricity this place would be racking up.

"What are we looking for exactly?" I ask him as I open an empty cabinet with each hand. "Why are there so many empty secret compartments?"

"We're looking for anything someone thought important enough to keep in a safe house for starters," he says gruffly as if I couldn't have asked a more foolish question. "Food, of course, even if you're too good for sardines like little miss fancy pants."

Maia rolls her eyes. If the Elder hadn't forgotten what prison food was like, he'd know we've had worse. Some people just don't like sardines. I know I'd settle for some crackers right now if I could stuff a handful in my mouth. A bottle of water to go with it wouldn't be so bad.

"After that," the Elder continues, his breath getting heavier as the night wears on us all. "We need exactly what Sheffield was complaining about when we entered. Rations, clothes, weapons.

Survival is our number one priority. We can't do anything for anyone if we're dead - or worse - captured."

I clear my throat. "Weapons?" I ask.

"What about them?" the Elder says roughly.

"That's not our way," I tell him. "We've never had weapons."

The Elder looks at me dead in the eyes. "Weapons have more than one purpose. No wonder you were captured so easily. You never learned half of what your father knew, did you?"

"Enough to get me this far," I snapped back. "But I never had to use weapons. Who did? We're a peaceful group. We've never done anything but promote peace. Yet they rounded us up like lost dogs and slammed us inside their kennel. So maybe I'm not a wilderness expert. But here I am, so why don't you quit your complaining and lead us like the wise sage my father said you were."

The Elder leaned back against a wall and took a deep breath. "Weapons," he says without apology, "are a vital tool in a survival situation. Not all animals scare off so easily, some might need to be shot through the heart or the head. And we could all use some protein if we can come across a proper target."

"The State hasn't allowed guns since long before we were rounded up," Sheffield reminds him.

"Guns aren't the only things that shoot," he says. "Do any of you know how to use a bow and arrow?"

"Anything that causes devastation," Wiley pipes up. "A nice little explosive tip can do a fair amount of damage."

"Good," says the Elder. "Maybe we'll find one here. Look for a knife, a dagger, or a machete. Anything with a blade to get us through thicker parts of the forest. Tools in case blowing something up isn't the best solution."

"The solution to what?" I ask him. "What are we even doing here? Do we have a plan or are we just waiting around to get captured again?"

"Do we have a plan?" the Elder chuckles.

"Well…do we?" Maia backs me up.

"President Shah has had his men looking for me since before most of you knew there was trouble for the Faithful," the Elder says with a scowl forming on his face. "You all remember the prison numbers on your uniforms, don't you? I was number zero zero zero zero zero one."

"Why?" Maia asks. "What did you do?"

The Elder sighs. "They wanted to find out what I knew," he shakes his head. "There was a time when we were great in numbers. The Faithful had influence in Ariel, all the way up to the president's palace. They listened to us. They confided in us. Then they turned on us when it became politically expedient."

"But why…you?" Maia clarifies. "What's so…"

"What's so special about me?" the Elder laughs until he has a short coughing fit. "I asked myself that every day as they poked and prodded me, looking for secrets I would die to protect. They must have thought my pride would have led me to turn on the Faithful. They thought I'd prefer power and prestige over truth. But that's not really how we operate, is it? None of us are all that important. Some of us just know where to get bread and water."

"You still haven't told us your plan," Sheffield said with a fierce stare.

"I know," the Elder stared back. "But you're not going to like it."

"Well out with it then," Sheffield demands without wavering.

"I'm going to need more than ten seconds to give the full answer," the Elder grumbles. "And I promise I'll get to it, but for now we need to keep working. That is, if you don't mind preparing for our next move. We're going to need as many supplies as we can gather here. Electronics, explosives, rations we can take on the go, weapons, and a lot more. We're going to need to search every little door in this place if we're going to find everything we need."

"Need for what exactly?" Maia interrupts. "What are we going to do with all these…things?"

The Elder looked to the heavens and says, "Take courage, if you have any, because we're going to break the other prisoners out of Justice Hall."

"Are you mad?" Sheffield screamed.

"How on earth could we even think of doing that?" Rafe asks as his brother Wiley's eyes shoot wide open."

"We are not going back there!" Sheffield angrily slams his fists against the wall. "I was there far too long. I can't go back. I won't go back."

"There are no other options," the Elder barks. "You've seen with your own eyes what the State has in store for those of us who are among the Faithful. We don't have many more options for safe houses.

We'll run out of rations before you know it. We have to break their system and find a way to tell the world about it before they catch us again. We have to strike at the heart of the people or we will be no more."

"He's right," I tell them, shaking my head in disgust. "The State won't stop at finding us. Killing us isn't enough for them anymore. Making an example out of us won't satisfy them. They're going to extinguish the Faithful from the strongest to the weakest. If there is truly any faith left in us…"

"Then we have to take down the system," Maia says, standing up to shake her fist. "We have to fight back."

"We were born for this," Wiley says shaking hands with his brother.

"I'll go," Felicity answers softly. "I have nothing else."

Sheffield shakes his head and says, "You're all nuts. You know that?"

"Better to be insane for a just cause than to be a coward," I stand firm.

"Fine," he says with his nostrils flared. "If that's it, then that's it. Everyone keep searching for supplies. The Elder can tell us his brilliant plan after we know what's been hidden in all these drawers."

The rest of us agree and spend the rest of the night searching the safe house from wall to wall in every room for supplies. I hope it's enough. I hope my father would be proud of me. I pray he's still alive.

Chapter Eleven

Disappeared

"He's gone," Rafe shouts.

"He can't be," Wiley says in disgust, not wanting to believe it, but knowing it to be true.

I clear my groggy eyes and see that everyone else has been gearing up for a busy day while I've been fast asleep. "Not again."

"Have we checked every room?" Maia cries out. "He can't have just disappeared without a trace."

The Elder must have been as tired as me. He shakes off the cobwebs and clears his throat. "He left in the middle of the night. He won't be back."

"You saw him?" Maia gasps. "And you didn't stop him?"

"He was never going to go with us," the Elder says, shrugging his shoulders as he pulls himself up to his feet. "We should be thankful he only took a dagger and a pack of rations with him on his way out. He must not have wanted to make too much noise."

"But you saw him?" I ask for clarification.

"I was still awake when he left," the Elder nods his head. "Working out some details. I do my best thinking when no one's bothering me."

"I thought you said you already had a plan," Maia says, throwing her hands up to her hair and streaking them back down.

"I do have a plan," the Elder says lowering his voice. "But we have to work with what we have, not what I wish we had. And we need options for when things don't go well. This is more art than science."

"We don't have much at all," Rafe says with Wiley nodding in agreement. "Are you sure this is the last safe house that's…safe?"

The Elder's eyes fade away and from the looks of it, he doesn't want to answer.

"There is another," the Elder finally admits. "And it has everything we need. But I…"

"What are we waiting for?" Maia asks.

"It has everything we need - but we have to go through hell to get there."

"We are already in hell," Maia says without skipping a beat. "We've been in hell ever since President Shah was elected…if you can call it an election. The Governor is even worse and he's supposed to be next in line if anything ever happens to him. I'm sick and tired of living in a prison - here or there it's all the same. Either we take care of business or we wait for the next noose to come along. I'm not going to waste away without a fight."

"Do you all agree?" asks the Elder.

I look around and have never seen more determined eyes in a

group of individuals in my life. I nod my head and say, "What are we waiting for?"

"Everyone take a pack," the Elder orders as a commanding officer would. "And from here on out, everyone does as I say, or we will all die a very terrible death. Every aspect of this rescue mission must be followed to the most precise detail. Everyone needs their own rations, though we are running low, and their own tools. We must go out a different way than how we came in. They'll be looking for us to come out of that first hatch."

"What other way is there?" I ask, assuming everyone else is as confused as I am.

"There's another hatch that leads to the street," the Elder suggests."

"The city?" Maia asks.

"But it's daylight now," I remind him. "Won't we be spotted?"

"Not exactly," he tells us. "But we are left with only one option. This safe house is built directly under a secret base that very few know about. They keep their vehicles directly above us. We're going to have to…"

"Steal a truck?" Rafe says with excitement. "Leave that to me."

"I was going to say sneak out," the Elder says with one eyebrow raised. "But I like the way you think. Does everyone have their packs? We need to leave immediately. We have no time to spare."

"Ready," I say as I slide a knife into the side pocket of my pack.

"Me too," says Maia as we watch the twins exchanging handshakes.

"Follow me then," the Elder says, his voice sturdy and resolute. "We have no time to waste."

He leads us to one of the rooms and points to a trap door above us that I hadn't given much thought to as we were checking for supplies.

"How are we supposed to climb through the ceiling?" I ask.

The Elder, the tallest of us all, simply slaps his hand up through the low hanging ceiling and we see a ladder slide back down like a magic trick.

"How'd you…never mind," I say as the Elder begins to make his climb with the rest of us following behind. Maia follows him and Felicity is next. Rafe and Wiley hop up the steps with ease. But I hear something.

"The front hatch!" I yell.

The Elder, without hesitation, shouts back, "Get up here now, now, now!"

I scamper up the rope ladder, losing my footing just once, and hurry to pull up the hatch door behind me as I lift myself through the ceiling.

"Close it quick!" the Elder commands. "We have to run." He isn't the fastest at his age, but he hustles through the corridor around the corner to where we find ourselves in a gigantic warehouse filled with cars, trucks, and even tanks."

"The tank!" shouts Wiley, his voice cackling through the biggest grin any of us has shown in days.

"You fool!" the Elder cuts off his thoughts immediately. "You think we can simply drive around the valley in a tank without causing suspicion? That truck over there! It's camouflaged and might have some supplies that we need."

Wiley's shoulders sink.

"Glad that's settled and all, but how do we get it out of here?" I ask.

"See that door over there?" the Elder says, pointing to a sliding slab of metal. "Rafe…I need you to hack into the system and open it up."

"Can do," Rafe replies. "But why is there no one here? Why is this place empty. It feels like a trap."

"It's not a trap," the Elder stops him before his thoughts carried him any further. "There's a reason why the safe house was built where it was and why I brought us here in the first place. This is where they keep excess stock when they don't need it. The State has plenty right now, but that's because they're building for something bigger. They know a revolt could happen at any point in time. Ariel is fragile. We need to break the system."

"Got it," Rafe shouts before running back to the truck we begin to pile into. "We have thirty seconds before it closes back up."

"Perfect," the Elder shouts. "Buckle up, it's going to be a bumpy ride."

Rafe barely makes it to a seat in the back before the Elder streaks out of the garage and makes his way out of the facility. The roads are empty and the skies are gray. Fields of dying weeds lie on either side of us as we race toward the nearest gate out of the village.

"We have to get out of here before word gets out on the radio," Rafe reminds us. "Won't be long before they notice a missing vehicle if they find out how we escaped."

"Doesn't matter," the Elder says as he checks for anyone following them. "We've got one of us on the inside."

"What do you mean one of us?" I ask as we pull up to the gate.

The guard stops us abruptly and shouts for us to show identification.

The Elder shows his face and shouts, "no time!"

The guard does a double-take, pivots, and slams his hand on the button to raise the gate.

We're free. But it won't last for long if we can't get to where we're going safely.

"Forty-five minute drive to where we're headed," the Elder says, his voice calming down as he adjusts his seat for a more comfortable ride. There are a hundred of these trucks on the road at any given point in time. They'll think we're headed to the capital, but we're taking a backroad to a place just outside the prison."

I sit back and consider falling asleep, though I know I should stay vigilant. It's a bumpy ride, the winding roads mostly made of rock and dirt, and the forest trees providing cover while we pass a set of smaller villages near the southern border of the region. I can tell we're taking the long way to avoid officers of the State, but I'm so hungry. I desperately want to get to the safe house and scour for more rations.

"Look what we have here," says Wiley, who has been digging through a compartment to his side.

"What's that?" the Elder asks earnestly.

"Enough explosives to blow up half the prison if we wanted to," he says with a big grin.

"That would be great," I tell him, "if we wanted to kill all the prisoners. But this is a rescue mission."

"I said if," Wiley reminds me, throwing his hands up in the air. "But I can get us into anything that my brother's hacking skills can't."

"And we're going to need every bit of skill the two of you can manage," the Elder tells them. "We're going to need everyone to be sharp and clever and…"

"And what?" I ask, remembering that I'm none of those things.

"And I think we're being followed," the Elder says quietly. "Hold on tight. I'm going to try to lose them."

We pick up speed faster than I thought the truck could handle. It hasn't been a busy day on the road, but the Elder is now weaving in and out of the few cars in our way and there's another truck like ours keeping pace with every turn.

"Wiley!" the Elder shouts. "Do something!"

"I'm on it!" Wiley cackles. "Hold this, brother."

Rafe grabs a box full of explosives as Wiley wraps a wire around it, lights it, and chucks it out the window. I plug my ears just in time as the road behind us explodes with dirt and chunks of pavement.

"Woooooo!" Wiley laughs hysterically.

But the Elder tells him to be quiet and hold on as he swerves the truck suddenly onto a dirt road that I never would have even noticed on such a trip if I hadn't suddenly found myself on it.

"This isn't quite what I had in mind when I woke up this morning!" the Elder shouts as we fly through a dusty trail and approach a darkened tunnel. "But I don't think they're going to find us now."

The Elder flips the truck lights on and slows the truck speed down to a pace where we can breathe easy. But there's no sign of life and no end of the tunnel in sight.

"Where are we?" I ask.

"It doesn't matter where we are," the Elder says. "It matters where we're going. This tunnel, long ignored by the State, will lead us straight to the last safe house anyone ever wants to visit."

"Then why are we going there?" Maia asks.

"Because it lies directly beneath the prison," the Elder explains. "Don't expect to see proper light until the time comes. I pray the generators are still working and someone left us enough food to sustain us until we're ready."

"Ready for what?" I ask.

"Do you think we're just going to waltz into Justice Hall and ask them for our friends back?" the Elder asks, shaking his head. "No. This is the most prestigious, if you want to call it that, or at least the most secure prison facility the State has in operation. This underground opening is the one way in without anyone noticing and it's the one small chance we have of breaking them free."

"How small of a chance?" Wiley asks. "What are we doing here if we're just walking into a losing fight?"

"Small," the Elder repeats. "But what chance do we have of

surviving out there in any other way? We not only have to free the prisoners, but we also must convince the world we're not the enemy. We have to show them that the State is falling apart and display how we can help them restore this nation to greatness."

"How on earth are we going to do that?" I press him. "We're nothing but a miserable group of nobodies with no power and limited skills. You think a couple of hacks and some fireworks are going to keep the prison guards at bay for long? What do you have up your sleeve that we don't know about?"

"You never listen, do you?" the Elder shouts as he slides the truck around a corner. "What have I been telling you over and over again? The Faithful used to have influence in the State. We used to have a name for ourselves that the people considered worthy of attention."

"And how does that help us now?" I demanded.

"Because I am called the Elder for a reason, you fool!" he defended himself. "Who do you think had access to the President? Why do you think he hates the Faithful so much now? Huh? It was me! This is…this…it's all my fault."

"Your fault?" Maia prodded him. "How could you-"

The Elder slowed the truck to a halt and flared his nostrils as he looked back at us.

"Everything that's happened to you, your family, your friends, it's all because of me," he said with an intense glare I had never seen before, not from him, not from anyone. "I was the President's most trusted counselor in Ariel. He came to me for everything, whether for national defense, domestic affairs, or which flavor of ice cream he should try. He sought my wisdom, he trusted me, confided in me, and then turned on me when I found out…"

"When you found out what?" I dared to ask him.

"I found out something about President Shah he didn't want the world to know," the Elder tells us.

"What was it?" I ask him.

The Elder shakes his head. "Something he didn't want to get out," he says. "Something personal. Something I told him was wrong, but he wouldn't listen to me."

"But why would he take it out on us?" Maia asks.

"It drove him mad," the Elder says without a doubt in his mind. "It's a strange thing, the human heart and its desires. It wants what it cannot have, though often a man might find a way to take it anyway, then decide for himself that it is right despite the counsel of his heart warring within him."

"Would you spit it out?" I ask, becoming frustrated with his half-answers.

"I suppose there's no harm now," he grumbles. "I discovered the President in an inappropriate relationship. I did not seek out this information, nor would I have had any business putting forth the information into the world, but when I confronted him on the matter he was afraid I was blackmailing him. He knew very well my beliefs and values and how they affected my response to his actions, but he had grown paranoid."

"So he took his grievance with you out on the Faithful?" I ask as I put all the information together while the words came out of my mouth.

"Now you're starting to get it," the Elder nods. "The President became enraged and illogical. It wasn't long before he distrusted any word I gave him, even if it were so simple a child could have given him such counsel, and so he thrust me out of my position."

"But there's more to it than that, isn't there?" Maia realizes. "You weren't just out of a job, you were the first of us thrown into prison for our beliefs as you said. What did you do to get put in the abomination above us?"

"I did the worst thing a man can do to a politician," the Elder says, his voice now getting sadder and softer. "I was interviewed for a radio station the day after I was fired from my position. The woman interviewing me asked why I was fired and I told the truth."

"Hang on," says Wiley. "Why wouldn't we have heard about all this?"

"Because it was a radio station owned by the State," the Elder shakes his head. "It wasn't a live interview, it was meant to be broadcast over the following weekend. Word spread quickly, from the show producers to the president. Bribes were paid, voices were silenced, and I was tossed in jail as a traitor. Finally, they did the same to everyone I ever cared about and many I never even knew."

"So it was you all along?" I asked as the Elder reaches for the pack by his side. "You turned the State against us?"

"Now you know the truth of the Elder," he says. "A wise man turned into a fool. I'd like to find redemption. I need your help."

"We're not here just to help you find forgiveness for your

mistakes," I tell him. "We're here because there are people up there in Justice Hall who need our help. My father, if he's still alive, is one of them. They're going to bring him back to the gallows as soon as they can."

"I meant I need your help with the door up there," says the Elder. "It gets jammed and a few extra hands on the lever will make it easier. Don't think for a second I believe this mission is all about me. I'm just an old man, mostly forgotten by the Faithful who remain."

"You're not forgotten," Maia says as she helps Felicity out of the truck. "Your name is whispered throughout the prison. The Elder did this. The Elder did that. I never knew of any of your mistakes. I don't know if you were right to do what you did or not. I'm no politician. But I do know you can begin to make up for it if we can get these people free."

Wiley, Rafe, and I help the Elder take hold of a giant metal wheel which takes all our combined efforts to nudge loose and spin the rusted door out of its position.

"No room for the truck," I shake my head.

"We would want to walk anyway," the Elder says. "There are some things in these halls we wouldn't want to shake loose with reckless driving."

"Like what?" I ask as he leads us through a darkened corridor. "And can we get some light?"

The Elder, who I can now hardly see, manages to feel his way around the walls until he can flick on a switch. It takes a minute or two to warm up, but the generator does its job and lights up the hallways.

"Will they notice all this electricity suddenly being used?" Rafe asks as the Elder ushers us from hallway to hallway.

"The State has bigger issues to worry about right now than the electric bill," the Elder scoffs. "That earthquake that let you all escape affected the capital and most of the surrounding region. They're going to be focused on getting the roads in order, the stadium resettled, and the people back to work."

"How much time do you think we have before they have things up and running?" I ask.

The Elder shakes his head. "Not much time at all. It'll take months before things can be back to the way they were, but people adapt, they work through difficulties, and the president will want to make a show of their strength and stability before too long. But we do have something going for us."

"What's that?" Maia asks as the Elder checks a door handle only to find it has been locked.

"You'll see in a minute," he answers. "Wiley, I need your assistance."

"I'm on it," Wiley answers. "But you might want to go around the corner if you like your body parts where they are."

No one thinks he's bluffing. We walk quickly around the corner while he snatches a small device from his pack, quickly plasters it to the door, and smacks a red button in the center.

Wiley runs around the corner like a rabbit scurrying to safety as the door is blasted open. Smoke, dust, and bits of wood fill the hallway. We wait for it to settle down, then the Elder runs through the smoke to reach for a fire extinguisher to put out the small flames left by the explosion. When the air clears, we understand what he meant by having something going for us.

"Welcome to the control room," says the Elder, still covering his mouth to protect his lungs. "It has…"

"Everything!" Rafe chortles. "Radio, satellite, high definition screens on every wall. This must connect to every major…"

"Don't get too excited," says the Elder. "Remember this place was deserted for a reason, not on accident. Nothing's going to be connected as it sits. I need you to do whatever you can to get us into the State's systems, especially the prison control tower."

"I'll get on it," Rafe tells him. "But I haven't eaten in a while. Do you think this place has any rations?"

"It will," says the Elder. "But we might have to search high and low for them."

"There was some stuff in that truck we brought," says Felicity.

"There was?" I nearly scream. "Why didn't you say something? We're all starving."

Felicity shrinks and doesn't want to answer.

"Lay off," says Maia. "Flick was scared like the rest of you. We'll go get the supplies and bring it back while you guys clear up this mess. I don't want to be breathing in fumes for the rest of the time we're down here."

"You're right," I say. "I'm sorry, Felicity, I just got excited."

"It's okay," she says, shrugging her shoulders.

"C'mon," says Maia.

Wiley helps me locate a janitor's closet in the hallway and we begin to clean the rubble from his handiwork. The Elder begins to show Rafe around the systems and where he thinks things might have been disconnected.

I'm doing what I can, but I don't feel like I'm much use to the team. This is too important. I have to find my worth. My father is somewhere up above in a cell waiting for the day when he will be hung from a rope. He could have been free from this. He could have escaped instead of focusing on telling me to run. He should have been the one helping out this team. I'm just another guy.

Maia and Felicity hand out rations and we gather around a circular desk that must have had a much more important function than a dinner table when it was first in use.

"You said you need us," I remind the Elder. "Well, we're all here, and we have nowhere else to go. I don't mean to speak for anyone else, but I believe we are all in on this mission. At some point, however, we are going to need to know the rest of your plan if we are going to execute it. So - what is it?"

The Elder, who had just put a cracker to his mouth, set it back down and focused our attention on his eyes.

"This isn't going to be easy," the Elder grimaces. "Every single one of you will be putting your lives in danger to accomplish our goal. I don't know if any of us will make it out alive. Still, this is the showdown we have been waiting for and I am going to need everyone here to do their part just the way I show you. I am going to train each of you to do exactly as needed to free the Faithful, corrupt President

Shah's grip on the State of Ariel, and bring the nation to an age of enlightenment."

"When do we start?" asks Maia.

"After we have something to eat," the Elder says, finally cracking a smile. "We're all going to need our strength to get us to past the finish line."

"I don't know what I have to offer this group," I admit. "But I'll give every ounce left of me to free the Faithful, to save my father."

Chapter Twelve

The Plan

"How many days?" Maia asks.

I wake up and rub my eyes. I must have dozed off for a few minutes after lunch.

"Two if we're lucky," the Elder suggests. "But I'm not counting on anything. We need to prepare as quickly as possible if we're going to give ourselves any chance for success."

"Where do we start?" I mumble as I try to push myself off the floor.

The Elder looks at me for a moment, then barks out, "Where do we stand, Rafe?"

"Just a minute and…I'm in," Rafe answers. "I can hear everything."

"And the other locations?" the Elder asks. "Are they all online?"

Rafe waves his hand dismissively, flips a few switches, then repeats the process several times. "A few glitches here and there, but mostly good. I'll work on them if and when they happen, but I'm receiving communications from the command stations clear as day."

"Good," the Elder commends him. "Then I need you to keep an ear out for what we discussed. The rest of you…you've got a lot to learn in a short time frame."

What they discussed? He's still leaving some of us in the dark.

"You three, over here," the Elder orders.

Maia, Felicity, Wiley, and I walk over to a table where the Elder has drawn out a rough schematic of the prison system from memory. He's no artist, but I spent enough time up there to recognize most of the rooms I had been able to access before we were isolated in our cells.

"How do we get up there?" I ask.

"The area where we are currently located has been shut down long enough that only the oldest guards even know it exists," says the Elder. "It's been left to decay, but a few of the Faithful found it to be… useful to our cause at times."

"Why wouldn't they at least have it destroyed or secured?" I ask. "How were we able to get down here so easily without alarms sounding up there?"

"Rafe isn't the only expert in electronics who has belonged to the Faithful," the Elder says bluntly. "We've had a number of things - well, let's just say that the guards up there aren't seeing what they think they're seeing. As far as they know, nothing down here has functioned for years, and no one comes to visit down here except for an occasional gopher."

"But they know we're out there somewhere," I remind him. "And after that truck followed us, they at least know the general area we're in now. Is there anything that could lead them here?"

"Not from the chatter I've been picking up," Rafe chimes in. "They think we're trying to flee the region altogether…they suspect we might have passed the southern border by now."

"And that wouldn't have been a bad idea," the Elder nods. "It would have been cowardly, perhaps, but I hope we're all past such aspirations."

"My father won't be freed by cowardice," I shake my head. "So how do we get up to the prison without detection?"

"That's the other reason why they aren't worried about what's down here," the Elder says, wincing. "The closer we get, the higher the security gets. It's not going to be easy. It's not going to be clean. We're going to have to…"

"Climb through the sewers?" Wiley asks before taking a deep breath.

"That's the simple part," the Elder frowns. "Disgusting, but simple, if your stomach can handle it."

"We haven't eaten much the last few months," Maia reminds him. "I don't think our stomachs are going to be any problem."

"I could use something to eat," Wiley suddenly remembers. Has anyone found anything good to…"

"We'll get to that," the Elder says. "You'll need your strength to climb through whatever mess has built up over the years. Now I need you to study these tunnels I've drawn out. Our best path is most likely the one that spirals around to an entry point. It's a longer path, but the door is easier to crack open than the others"

"Is it locked?" I ask.

"It's a prison," the Elder says flatly. "Every door is locked in a prison, even the garbage chute. That's why we're so glad you're around, Wiley."

Wiley's face lights up, but his eyes are still scouring for where he might find a box of crackers or anything that hasn't rotted away.

"Now, we're not likely to find anyone in the area if we can manage to get up there in the middle of the night as I plan," says the Elder. "So if you need to make a little noise with this one, that's okay. But after that, we're going to need precision and timing down to the last detail."

"Where do we go from there?" I ask. "Getting into prison isn't so hard, we've all done that, but how do we get out with the rest of the Faithful intact?"

The Elder then takes us through the schematics and shows us room by room where the guards are known to be located, why it was designed the way it was, and the best path to get to the prisoners and lead them to safety.

When the Elder finishes, no one says a word for a long time, each calculating in our own minds the likelihood that a group of six escaped prisoners have the guts, the knowledge, and the luck to pull off such a magnificent feat.

"I don't suppose you know how to trigger an earthquake at just the right time, do you?" I ask as I rub my chin. "I don't know how else we're going to pull all this off without getting ourselves back in line for execution."

"It does sound a little…" Wiley shakes his head as he tries to agree with me politely. "What are the odds we can pull this off?"

"It's not for the faint of heart," the Elder affirms. "And I can't promise any of you that we will succeed. If you all want to hang out here and die when the rations run out, then that's an option we can put on the table. If you want to make a run for it in that government truck we stole, well, we can hop in there and see how far we get before we run out of gas. But if you…"

"No!" I say, slamming my fists on the table. "I don't care if there's a one percent chance of survival. I don't care if I have to do it alone. My father is up there with a bunch of other people that don't deserve to die for believing the truth. I'm going up there no matter how foolish it might seem. Though none go with me, I will still go. Just tell me the best path."

"This is the best path," the Elder sighs. "I've been over it in my head every day since the moment I first escaped. It's the most dangerous, but it is also our best chance of success. If we are meant to succeed, then we will succeed. If we are meant to fail, then it is because it must be so."

"Then it's time to prepare," I say, though my thoughts are drifting from me as I think of what my father must be thinking. Does he know I made it out of the stadium? Did they lie to him? Did they tell him we died just to watch him lose all purpose and hope? Would he have believed them? If I know him, he's more worried about me than about himself, which is why I'm doing what I'm doing. I might not be as smart and cunning as my father, but I can at least try to act like him.

The Elder waves his arm and says, "Maia and Felicity, you two follow me. I'll start with your training. Wiley and Niko, you two can scrounge up some rations for the rest of us while you wait."

"Looks like we're partners, then," Wiley says as he puts his arm over my shoulder. "Always thought it would be Rafe that would be next to me in these situations, but I understand why the Elder wants him down here in the command center."

"He's a hard guy to replace," I admit to him. Rafe and Wiley have impressed me with their knowledge in cracking into systems, each in their own way. I wonder how they were ever captured in the first place, but that's not the thing most of us like to talk about. Maybe one day, if we get out of this alive, if the Elder's plan works like we hope it does, then we'll share our stories. But now is not the time to think of past failures.

"It's okay, Niko," Wiley says. "I know you've got it in you. You survived just like the rest of us. That doesn't happen by accident."

"It does seem strange to me," I say as we walk through the corridors to where the Elder believes we'll find the best rations.

"What's that?" Wiley asks, opening the door and swinging it wide open.

"Did you think about who escaped during the earthquake?" I ask. "It was all the young ones. I wonder why that was."

"Young legs, perhaps?" Wiley suggested.

"Maybe," I shrug. "Or were we of less concern to them than those with more experience. Maybe they think we're not really capable of much on the run. If I were them, that's what I'd be telling the people, that they got people like my father because they were the most dangerous."

"I guess we get to prove them wrong," Wiley nods. "It doesn't really matter if anyone believes in us. It matters what we believe."

We begin to rummage through the cabinets of the supply room and realize that while the Elder had made a correct assumption about this room having the rations we need, the supplies were little more than the basic necessities. Water, crackers, canned tuna, some beans. Not the meal I was hoping for, but the kind I should have expected, and there's plenty of it to keep us going.

"You're not a cook, are you?" I ask.

"Afraid not," Wiley says shaking his head. "But I can get a fire going in a pinch. At least we won't have to eat those beans raw."

"Well, that's something," I say. "Not sure there's much even the best cook could do with these ingredients anyway. I don't remember my mother ever talking about preparing beans and tuna with crackers when I was growing up."

"Your mother was a cook?" Wiley asks as he begins to pile the rations into my outstretched arms. "Any good?"

"She was the best," I tell him, knowing that it's the first thing to really cause me to smile in months. "You should have tasted the things she could whip up with the simplest ingredients. We never had all that much to spend on food when I was young, but she would pick up a few items at the market and turn it into something like you hear about from one of those fancy restaurants for the wealthy."

"So you're saying it was better than prison food?" Wiley asks as he slaps me on the back and we make our way to the command center. "Wish I could try it someday."

I try not to think about my mother too much. It hurts not knowing where she's been all these years. I've feared the worst, that she was locked up, tortured, and ultimately executed. I take little comfort in the fact that she never made an appearance on Independence Day. I don't know if the State ever thought of her as the threat they considered my father. Whatever they've done, I hope she was never treated the way we were."

"That didn't take long," Rafe shouts as he swivels around in a worn-down, black leather chair that squeaks whenever he shifts his weight. "Good thing…we don't have much of it to spare."

"Did you learn something?" his brother asks him immediately.

"Two days," Rafe says as he scratches his forehead. "They're cleaning up what's left of the debris from the earthquake. The stadium will be ready tomorrow, the roads will be clear the next day. They're going to do a makeup session for Independence Day."

"Executions?" I choke on my own word as it comes out.

"Twelve," Rafe says softly. "The six who were recaptured, plus six to replace us. They've been telling everyone that we'll get what's coming to us, one way or another, and they're certain we're in no condition to be an immediate threat to the citizens of Ariel or the surrounding nations."

"That's what they want people to think," the Elder says. "But they'll be looking for us until they have each of our heads in a bucket. We're going to make it either very easy or very difficult for them in the next few days."

"Let's pray it's difficult," Rafe says as he swings his chair back around. "Let me know when the food's ready!"

Wiley lights up a flare and uses it to spark the kindling we had fashioned out of a few broken cabinets from the corner of the room.

"There aren't...sprinklers in here are there?" I ask.

"Would have gone off by now," the Elder claims. "But the water has been cut off for years. That's not something we're going to have to worry about. I'm more concerned with Wiley smoking us out of the one room down here that's of any use to us."

"It's all under control," he assures us. "This isn't my first fire, you know."

"You got me there," the Elder shrugs. "And I'm counting on that. I need you to be every bit of an expert on explosives that you seem to think you are. I wish we had months to train for this heist, but we only have the time we have been given."

"You won't have to worry about the explosives," Wiley says. "But none of us know much about this prison beyond the bars of our cells and a few hallways they pushed us through. We need to know the ins and outs of this place or we're going to find ourselves stuck in a dead-end or electrocuted by secret traps."

"Well, that's what we're going over the rest of the day," the Elder says as we begin to prepare our meal. "And you won't have to worry about going down any dead ends as long as you stick to the plan. I need you to execute everything to the smallest detail. We can't afford mistakes."

"Execute might be a poor choice of words," Maia tells him as she notices Felicity shaking. "Remember why we're doing this. People are counting on us, even though they don't know it. This isn't some silly war game where we win a trophy. This is life or death."

We are all aware of that, of course, but her words silence the room. Most of us don't know each other that well, but we are putting our lives in each other's hands. We don't know if there will be another miracle to rescue the Faithful from the next execution.

"What do you have the girls doing?" I ask the Elder before jamming a cracker in my mouth.

"I need them to acquire some objects for me by stealth," he tells us. "Felicity already proved herself worthy in this manner. Maia knows how to follow a path. If we are to free the prisoners and begin a revolution, I need them to make their way into a supply cabinet near the prison's offices. It won't be easy, even at night, but there are ways around this prison known by only a few."

"A revolution?" Wiley asks. "I know the Faithful can't keep living like this, always on the run, praying to keep away from the gallows, but how are we going to start a revolution? There are so few of us."

"And we have such little power and influence," I add. "Even if we free every prisoner in Justice Hall, they're going to round many of them back up. Tell me there's more to your plan."

"The people need to see the truth," the Elder nods. "And thanks to Rafe's infiltration of their communications, we are going to be able to tell the world of our plight, our true beliefs, and the lies of the State. But we have to time things perfectly or they'll never know."

"And where do we come in?" I ask as I point to Wiley, then back to myself. "I know what he can do, but I don't know anything about explosives, and any noise will cause guards to come running."

"Precisely," the Elder says. "You wouldn't know how to stay quiet if your mouth was stapled shut and your feet were made from feathers. Which is why I need you two to confuse the guards. You're going to set up a series of distracting explosions that will divert their attention."

"Won't that cause a panic?" Wiley asks. "Won't it cause them to shut down the entire system? No one would be able to escape if every door in the prison is put on lockdown."

"Did you forget about me so soon, brother?" Rafe shouts from his command.

"Rafe is staying down here to give us directions as we go," says the Elder. "I retrieved some communication earpieces at the last safe house. You will each wear one and listen for instructions as we maneuver our way to our eventual destination. Rafe will be in our ears the entire time, making sure we don't run into any unforeseen problems. He will also be hacking into the system to make sure certain doors work properly…and others don't work at all."

"Great," I say. "Then show us where to go."

"I will," he says. "But let's get something to eat first. I don't know about all of you, but I'm starving."

It was only at this that I remembered how we all looked. We aren't well-fed spies who have been dining at fancy restaurants. We aren't even poverty-stricken peasants living off our own modest income. We have all been at death's doorstep. I don't know how we've managed to make it this far without constantly collapsing.

"If we get out of this…" I start to contemplate.

"When we get out of this," Maia says confidently.

"I'm going to learn how to cook like my mother did," I say. "Maybe find a place to live far out in the country. Away from this madness. You all can come over any time you like for some home cooking."

"I think I'd like that," Wiley tells me. "Anything has to be better than this rat food."

"I'm not sure the rats would touch this stuff," Felicity says.

"The girl speaks!" the Elder laughs.

"I talk plenty," she says. "At least I used to. But my heart hurts too much to talk the way I once did."

"You miss your family?" I ask.

"Of course I do," she says. "But it's not that. Not entirely. It's just…the world we live in. It isn't right. I don't understand how people can live with what they're doing to us. They ripped us away from our families, they shut us up in prison and beat us, and if it weren't for the earthquake we'd all be dead already. How can they live with themselves?"

The Elder shakes his head. "Those who are blind, do not know what they can't see. They might have ideas, they have some understanding of the world around them, but nothing can replace true sight. The State has blinded these people from reality. They think us to be so evil that killing us is no worse than stepping on a spider. No one feels sorry for the spider. We need to open their eyes. That's what this is all about."

"I'm all for it," I say softly. "But how will freeing all the criminals accomplish that? I'll do anything to help them escape if it will work, but I don't understand how we're going to do anything but flee."

"It took me years to figure out that part of the equation," said the Elder. "And though I hate how this is the way it must be done, it is the only plan I've been able to engineer that could work the way we need it to. If you do as I have instructed, if you follow everything I say down to the last detail, then we have a chance to tell the world our story. It's complicated, and it won't happen without death trailing us at every turn, but I need you to trust me. We will have a chance to tell the world our story. We will have our shot at freedom."

I've never heard such a cryptic answer, but I can tell I'm not going to receive further clarification, so I hold onto the only things I have left, a shred of hope and the sheer determination to get it done. My father always spoke so highly of the Elder, but now I realize he always spoke of him in mysteries and partial stories. If he had my father's trust, then I'm going to have to give him mine as well.

"So it is settled," I say as I look around at the others, who all appear to be handling their reservations. "Our lives and theirs are in your hands. None of us have the experience you do. None of us have a better plan in mind. If we're going to do this, I still need to know one thing…is everyone all in?"

The room is silent for a moment. I'm not the only one with mixed feelings. Our lives are at stake. We could all be dead in two days. I've come to grips with that before, and so have they, but that doesn't make it any easier the second time around.

"I don't know anyone up there," says Maia. "I couldn't tell you any of their names. I hardly remember their faces. But as far as I'm concerned, those are our brothers and sisters. If we left them to die, then how will we live for the rest of our days, even if we were to escape and live to be a hundred and twenty years old?"

"I'm…" Felicity hesitates. "I'm scared. But you are all I have now. I will go."

"Let's blow some stuff up, shall we?" says Wiley. "Rafe?"

"If you're all done with your little group chat over there…" Rafe answers with a swivel of his chair. "I've got some bad news. They've moved the executions up to tomorrow. And if you thought Independence Day was a dreadful time…I think President Shah is about to make some changes to make tomorrow even worse."

I can feel every strand of hair stand up on my arms. My hands and feet are suddenly frigid. My eyes are wide open. Rafe has my full attention.

"Details," the Elder orders.

"You're not going to like it," Rafe shakes his head. "But I think they've got something more gruesome in mind than the gallows. Every television crew in the world will be there. They want everyone to see the power of the State, their utter dominance, and the complete destruction of our people."

"How does this affect what I've told you?" the Elder asks urgently.

"We've lost the rest of our prep time," Rafe says. "We need to go tonight."

"We're not ready," I said.

"A crash course will have to do," the Elder says. "You can toss your plates aside. We've had our fill. If this goes according to plan, we'll either be dead or eating real food again this time tomorrow."

"Where do we start?" I ask, but the Elder isn't listening as he runs over to Rafe and snags a notebook he had given him.

"I'll bring it back," he says bluntly and returns to us. "According to the clock, we have two hours to get ready, then we make our ascent."

"It won't even be dark outside yet," I say.

"It's not an easy trip," he reminds us. "We have to go slow. We have to be careful. We need to keep our eyes open for surprises every step of the way. We're going to need all the time we have to get there by morning."

The Elder goes on for two hours, giving us intense, detailed instructions, making us repeat each step over and over again like children so we won't forget a single move. This is an operation destined to fail if we make a single small mistake.

None of us lose focus. No one here is so foolish to think we can get away with making a single error. I know I couldn't live with myself if I were the one who made it all go wrong. Then again, if that's the case, I won't have to.

Chapter Thirteen

Home

My legs bounce up and down as I stare into the recesses of my mind. My hands are folded over my eyes, but I'm too distracted by my thoughts to focus my prayers on the mission that awaits us.

We're not prepared. Malnourished, sleep-deprived, and barely trained for the task at hand. At least the others seem to have some level of skill or expertise for their assignments. What am I? I'm nothing. I'm no one. Just the son of a great man, desperate to release him from his chains, to honor a true hero.

I spent years under his tutelage. He thought he was training me to take over his work, but I was little more than a shadow, never close to fulfilling all he had promised I would become. I wanted to be like him more than anything, but at the same time everything he was as a man scared me. Because it wasn't me.

Now here I am, surrounded by a small remnant of the Faithful, and of what use to them am I?

"You got this far," I hear a quiet voice. It's Maia. She had been sitting next to me for the past half hour as we all sat silently and waited for the right time to begin our mission. "Do you really think a useless person could have made it here?"

"Are you talking to me?" I say. "Wait, have I been talking out loud this entire time?"

"Only a little bit," she said. "Mumbling, mostly. I don't know what's going on in your mind, but I did hear you mutter something about being useless, and that can't be true. You escaped. You found the Elder and the two of you found us. If it weren't for that, we wouldn't be here together. The rest of us would have been stuck with that coward, Sheffield."

"We don't know he's a coward," I say. "I mean, probably, but we don't why he left for sure."

"No," she says. "But I've always been pretty good at reading people. At least I think so. Of course, the past couple of days have been the first I've been around people for a while."

"Except the guards," I remind her.

"Barely people," she says. "Monsters, most of them."

"No different than the rest of us," I shake my head. "If it weren't for the faith, anyway, we'd be no different than them. Even now, I have my moments. Sometimes I just want to…"

"I know," she says. "But after a few months in those cells up there, it's hard to remember better times. It's hard to keep the faith when there's no one around to remind you, to tell you to keep your head on straight. I could have been one of those traitors if it weren't for…"

"Your heart," I tell her. "My father always told me that the heart would always reveal its true self when faced with the greatest adversity. You had every opportunity, I'm sure, to recant."

"True," she said. "But so did Sheffield. And look at what he did. It took him longer than most, but he ran."

"That's why I still have hope for him," I tell her. "Maybe it's misguided, maybe he is a traitor like you said, but I hope he just had another plan in mind."

Maia smirks. "So your mama was a cook and your papa was out in the field. Sounds like you had it pretty good before all this."

"Everyone has their struggles," I tell her. "How'd you get into this mess?"

Maia shakes her head. "The hard way," she answers with a half-smile betrayed by downcast eyes. "I had a family too, once, but I was taken from them. The State said I was in trouble, or that I was trouble, I never did get the same answer twice. I had a little sister, not much older than Felicity, I guess that's why I'm so protective of her. I don't want to lose anyone else. The Faithful is the closest thing to a family I have these days."

"Are they still out there, somewhere?" I ask her before putting my hand to my mouth, realizing it could be a touchy subject.

"I hope so," she says. "But it's not like any of us got visitors in those cells, you know. Maybe they saw me on the news. I hope so. Maybe they know I escaped. I hope I don't disappoint them."

"You won't," I tell her. "And I hope to meet them someday if this plan works the way the Elder says it will."

"Ahem," the Elder interrupts us. "It is almost time for us to go. I want you all to double-check your packs. Make sure you have everything on the list. Then take one more good look at the schematics of the prison I have drawn upon the table over there. We aren't going to take that with us. If someone makes a mistake and gets caught, we don't want them to discover what the rest of us are up to."

"Five minutes until I need everyone lined up at the hatch," Rafe instructs us. "I won't have time for idle chat when you're up there, but I want you to know that I expect to see you on the other side of this, and I'll be in your ear the entire way. Listen to what I say and we have a better chance of pulling this off. Godspeed."

"One more thing," I say. "It's time for you to be the leader I've always heard about."

The Elder looks back at me with a grimace.

"No, I don't mean as the wise man, or the political expert, or the tactician. No, my father spoke of you often, and never did he mention any of that. He told me about how you led the Faithful through thick and thin, when things were good and when things were bad. It's time for you to remember what got you that reputation."

The Elder stares back at me. I don't know if he's going to punch me or tackle me, but he doesn't look happy about his choices.

"I know," he finally confesses. "So if you have the ears for one more speech from an old man, please hear this one."

"Time's ticking," Rafe reminds us.

"Go ahead," says Maia.

"I've lived a long, terrible life," says the Elder, his eyes tired and gray. "I spent many of those years in service to the Faithful, and it was a great joy to work alongside people like Niko's father and mother. I'm sorry I haven't gotten to know the five of you as well as I would have liked. If things go according to plan, perhaps there will still be time. I want you to remember one thing, no matter what happens. Keep your eyes on the King. The President will do whatever he can to tear us apart, but the Faithful will always be loyal to the King."

"It's time," says Rafe. "Everyone to your positions!"

"Focus," says the Elder. "The King will guide your path."

Maia and Felicity line up first. There's a ladder that goes twenty feet up before Maia has to open the hatch. She struggles, but it loosens, and they vanish without a goodbye. There's no time for pleasantries. Everyone has their mission.

"Your turn," the Elder says to Wiley and me. "The King will guide your path."

It's been a long time since I've heard that phrase. Saying it out loud would lead to the harshest beatings Justice Hall had to offer.

I nod my head and climb the ladder first, Wiley right behind me, each of us carrying a pack of various explosives for him to set off throughout the night and into the morning. But it's a long, slow climb to get to where we're going.

I turn on my flashlight. It's dim, but it's enough to get us where we're going. Maia and Felicity take a right, and if things go according to plan, we won't see them until the end. I lead Wiley to the left and begin our ascent.

"All this work," I tell Wiley. "And we're climbing through the sewers to get back to our cells."

"Thought we'd be dead by now anyway," Wiley says as we adjust to the smell of the catacombs. "But now we have a chance to do something for the Faithful that no one else can. And I get to make a few fireworks go off while we're at it. If this is how we go, it's gotta be better than Independence Day."

I'm not sure I agree with him. Independence Day was supposed to be humiliating, but it would have been quick and relatively painless. I don't know what tortures they might send our way if we are recaptured.

It isn't long before we hit our first marker. I hand Wiley one of the explosives from my bag and he carefully wraps it around a pipe with a thin line of string. "Back up," he tells me. "I've only got a few seconds to get to cover when this blows."

I slide back down through the grimy soot we'd been creeping up and he soon follows. Bang! That should clear a path for us to the lower levels of the prison which are still operational. It will still take us a while to get there as we muck our way through the sludge that has built up over the years.

"Team Two is all clear," says Rafe. I jump back and my reflexes make me slap the side of my face. I'd half-forgotten he was going to be in our ear until he finally broke his radio silence. No word on Maia and Felicity. The Elder told us not to expect progress on his part of the mission until the end. I don't know why he keeps his secrets, but my father trusted him, so I've decided to trust him too.

"I'm sorry it's not your brother on this mission with you," I tell Wiley. "I'm sure it would have been easier."

"Nah," he says. "Rafe is better down there observing everything. He always slows me down anyway. He makes precise calculations, I just like to light things up. We have our own ways. Nice to have some different company for a change."

"I don't know who designed this place," I say as we slink our way up step by step, "but they sure could've come up with an easier system to get to the first floor."

"I'm not sure this is the path that was meant to be taken," he laughs. "This is just the one that keeps us hidden."

"Team One, abort! Team One, abort!"

"What's that?" I ask Wiley. "What's happening?"

"I don't know!" he freezes. "These are one-way radios. We can't communicate."

"What do we do?" I shake him.

"Were they caught?" he asks.

"I don't know," I tell him. "I don't know what to do. Let's just keep going until…"

"Team One, you're clear. Go to Plan B," says Rafe. "I repeat, go to Plan B. I don't think they saw you, but it doesn't look to be a safe path."

"Breathe," I tell Wiley. "Breathe. They're okay. We need to continue."

Wiley looks back at me and nods, but he's still recovering.

"Just got real, didn't it?" I ask him, but he remains silent. "I know. I felt it too. But we need to gather all the courage we have to continue. We must act as though we are already dead, so we can live without fear, and act according to the knowledge the Faithful will be rewarded when all has come to the end."

"You're…you're right," he says, though his body is violently disagreeing with his words.

"Team Two, you are approaching your second target," Rafe tells us. "Breathe easy, guys, everyone is still on schedule. I never said this would be easy, but I need you to stay focused."

I take a deep breath and see Wiley do the same.

"Compose yourself," I tell him as I put my arm on his shoulder. "We need you. We trust you. There's the target right there, that green metal box on the wall."

Wiley rubs his hands over his face and resets his mind. "You're right," he says, settling himself. "If we die, we die, but let's try to live, huh?"

"That's a good idea," I tell him. "I prefer it that way, at least. What do we need to do here?"

"Won't take much," Wiley explains. "We're not trying to blow it to smithereens, we just need the security system to go down long enough for Team One to get past their next checkpoint. Take care of this for me."

Wiley hands me the explosive, and though I'm not an expert like he is, I know what to do with this one. I take a sticky, tar-like substance from my pack, slap it on the back of the bomb, and slam it up against the electrical panel.

"Run!" Wiley shouts as I slap a little red button. He doesn't have to tell me twice. I shuffle as quickly as I can behind him and around a corner. I close my eyes and cover my ears until I feel a blast of air behind me. "That should do it, but we have to move fast to our next target."

"Let's roll," I tell him, well remembering the Elder's instructions. Funny thing, when my life is on the line, it's easier to focus. Still, I hope to get out of this habit someday. "Over there, I see the next panel."

We run up to the panel and Wiley shakes his head. "This isn't it," he says.

"What do you mean?" I ask him. "It looks the same as the one the Elder told us about, and it's in the corner just like on the map."

"No," Wiley tells me. "Look, these wires aren't even connected. I think someone must have changed the…"

"Team Two, Team Two, listen up!" Rafe shouts. "The next panel is a trap, don't touch it!"

"A trap?" I ask, but Rafe can't hear me.

"I knew something was fishy," Wiley tells me. "But what now?"

"Team One, hold your position," Rafe orders. "Elder, I need you to do the thing we discussed."

"The thing?" Wiley and I say to each other.

"Team Two, the real wire should be through a door down the hall. Watch your step, but there shouldn't be any guards present. I'm going to trigger a false alarm on the south side of the courtyard around the prison. This will give you ten minutes to get to your final waiting positions."

"This is it, isn't it?" Wiley asks as we walk side by side down a dark corridor to where we see a small, unremarkable box in the corner next to the door. "Once we get to the next mark, there's no turning back."

"There never was any turning back," I tell him. "This isn't the route we asked for, but it's the life we chose, and all the freedom in the world isn't worth the lie of security the State has sold to the people."

"I know," Wiley says as he pulls out another explosive. "My brother and I - we've lost it all before. It was long before we were rounded up by the State's thugs. Our parents, our sister, our friends, they all abandoned us when they found out we were among the Faithful. They didn't understand why anyone would choose to live this life, to throw away all they thought they had in life. I know they're out there, somewhere, and I hope somehow our message gets to them and changes their mind. But even if it doesn't, I know of no other way to go."

"Run," I laugh as if he didn't know what to do after he set off the bomb. We duck behind a set of matching pillars fifty paces down the hall.

"We're going to have to crawl through that hole in the wall," Wiley complains. "At least we haven't been overeating lately."

"Speak for yourself," I tell him as we get down on our knees. "I had at least two dozen crackers this morning. Went straight to my stomach."

"Guess you'll just have to suck it in," Wiley grins as he goes through first.

I follow, and for the first time since we began, I have to compose myself. The bright lights of the prison hallways leave little room for lurking in the shadows. If Rafe's diversion didn't work, we're dead men.

"To the left," Wiley says, shaking me out of my glaze. "We don't have much time. Run, but be quiet."

"The girls must be safe," I say mostly to myself. "We haven't heard anything otherwise. The Elder too, I hope, though we don't know what he is really trying to do. I don't know why he kept his part secret."

"I have a hunch," Wiley tells me as we reach a set of double doors. He breaks them open in less than a minute with a simple pick from his pocket. "I don't think we're gonna like it if my hunch is right."

"What's your - never mind, we need to hurry to that door down the way," I remind him as we pick up our pace for a sprint to the finish.

"That's it, fellas," Rafe says in our ears. "You jam the system on the wall there. I'll see if I can work my magic."

"Can't get it open," Wiley tells me. "Help me with this?"

"Watch this," I say as I lift my left leg and shove it as hard as I can into the panel. "A little something I learned from my mom."

"What kind of cooking did you say she does?" Wiley asks me, but his face is too in focus to smile at his own quip. While the rest of his detonations were simple, he only had one shot at making this one work, and it has to be precise. "Hold onto the dynamite while I strap it in. Good. Now we just have to stretch out this cord a bit…and…run!"

It feels good to run. My leg still hurts a little, but it's little more than an annoyance. We spent months in those cells, nearly left to rot, only brought outside to breathe what was supposed to be our last bits of oxygen. To be running like this, to be joking, to be in the middle of this master plan to free the Faithful…it felt strange, but nice."

"Team One!" Rafe shouts in our ears. "Team One, this is your chance to smash that button and hightail it out of there!"

"What about us?" I ask Wiley.

"Come to think of it," Wiley scratches his head. "I don't think the Elder told us where to go after this…he just said…"

"Trust me," I remember. "He told us to have faith."

Then we hear a clang and turn around. Then another, and another, followed by dozens in a row. Every cell door in the entire prison has been opened.

"Attention!" says a voice over the intercom. "Your guards have been isolated and contained. You are free to escape. This is your only chance. Be Faithful until the end."

"Run!" I yell.

"Where?" Wiley shouts back.

"That way!" I tell him over the sudden clamor. "It leads to the north entrance. Rafe said he sent the guards to the south. That has to be the way!"

Everything becomes a blur to me as we run through the halls of the prison, the place we were forced to call home for so many months, the place where we were hidden until the day they decided it was time for us to die.

We approach the first set of cells. The doors have all swung open.

Prisoners have already fled. I can hear them running away in the distance, but I can't see them. "They're going to cause a bottleneck at the front gate," I tell Wiley.

"How many prisoners are normally in here?" Wiley asks. "We didn't get much walking around time."

"It has to be…hundreds," I guess. "Maybe thousands. And we're going to be last in line to get out."

"Let's go," Wiley says. "We don't know when those guards are going to get out of whatever trap my brother set for them."

Wiley turns around and runs toward the exit. I follow a few feet behind him, my legs now getting heavy, my breath getting shorter with every stride, but my eyes wide and focused like never before.

"How much further?" Wiley asks. "I've never been down this way."

"Me Either," I tell him. "It can't be too far. It's…oh no."

We reach the front doors, which have swung wide open, but the courtyard is filled to the brim with prisoners, not all of whom were political prisoners of the State, and few of whom are of the Faithful.

"They're in a panic," I shout over the tumult of those trying to push their way through the narrow gate that leads to freedom.

I look up and see a helicopter coming into view. I look back down and see prisoners escaping by the dozen. They're going to make it out, we're all going to escape these walls, but for how long?

"The State already knows what we've done," Wiley shouts. "They're going to know it's us."

"I know!" I yell back as we approach the throngs of people trying to push their way to the front.

"Team One, Team Two, when you get past the gate, take a sharp left around the prison walls. I'll meet you with the truck in ten minutes. We don't have much time. This is Rafe signing off."

"Ten minutes?" I shout. "We've got to get through this line."

Like the others, Wiley and I begin to squeeze our way through the crowd. Unlike the others, we've had a few meals in the last couple of days, and we're stronger than them. We easily duck and dodge through to the front of the line, shove our way through the gate, and gallop around the wall.

"Left!" I remind Wiley, but he was already turning that way.

I see the crowd and they're heading in every direction. They're lost, running to and fro without order, desperate to find a hiding place before the State sends reinforcements. I wonder if all this work will be for naught. Have we made things worse in the long run?

"I see the girls!" Wiley shouts. "They made it out!"

They spot us and wave us over to where they're standing. A truck in the distance is gliding across the dirt layers surrounding the prison. I turn around as I hear two more helicopters joining the first. The sirens begin to sound. They're coming for us.

"Get in!" we hear Rafe screaming at the top of his lungs. "We have to go now!"

"Where are we going?" I yell over the sirens and helicopter blades.

"The Elder gave me a location," he yells. "This isn't over. Not even close. This was only the beginning of the Elder's plan."

Rafe speeds off the moment we are all inside.

"I'm so glad you're safe," Maia says.

"So far," I tell her. "But I…I don't know what exactly we've accomplished. The State's going to round most of them up within the hour. There are only so many places to run from here. I didn't see my father inside. I don't…I don't know if he's going to make it out of this alive."

"He will," she says. "You have to know that."

I nod my head instinctively. I don't know why, but I believe she's right. My father has always been the bravest, cleverest, most cunning man I have ever known. If anyone can find a way out of this, it's him.

"Where are we headed?" Wiley asks his brother.

"We're headed home," Rafe yells.

Wiley shakes his head. "Home? You can't mean…"

"Afraid so," Rafe yells as we veer into the thick woods that we went through to get back to the prison in the first place.

"What's home?" I shout. "What do you mean?"

"Did we ever tell you where we're from?" Wiley asks me.

"No," I shake my head. "What's this about?"

"The reason Rafe and I know so much about these things, the reason we have these skills is that we grew up in the capital," he tells me. "Not just the capital…the presidential palace. That's why we were caught so easily. The President found out we were part of the Faithful and tossed us in that prison. Our family did nothing to stand in the way. They sided with him. We sided with the Faithful."

"So that means…" Maia gasps.

"We're going home," Wiley says. "And the Elder will meet us

there. This was no mere escape. This is our last stand."

"It was a diversion all along," Rafe confirms as he maneuvers through a winding dirt road. "The Elder needs an audience with the president and he wants the whole world to witness. We're going to be right there with him, side by side, to tell the entire world of our condition, of what they have put us through, and why the Faithful will never die."

Chapter Fourteen

A Technical Malfunction

"There it is," Maia says. "The Capitol. When I was a kid, I always wanted to come here, to see how the government was run, to witness law and order take place. I never dreamed…"

She didn't have to finish that thought. We knew what she meant. I gaze my eyes toward the mansion as Rafe slows the truck down to a less noticeable pace. It's a truly magnificent set of buildings with white pillars extending high in the air, the State's flag waving proudly above the dome in the center of the palace itself, a monument built to be the place where lawmakers once protected our freedoms. Now it's a cesspool for craven politicians who spend their days looking to take ours away.

"There was a time when it was a place worthy of its splendor," Wiley says, his typical smirk replaced with a scowl. "Growing up, there were good people in that house, people that wanted to do what was right for everyone, no matter what they believed or looked like. I disagreed with many of them on important concepts, but I never dreamed it would come to this. The world changed in a hurry."

"How are we supposed to get in?" I ask. "Another elaborate series of traps and explosives?"

Rafe brings the truck to a complete halt. "Afraid not," he says. "You see that gate in front there? The one with a top-level security agent operating the gate?"

"You can't mean…" I start to ask, but we're interrupted by company.

"It's the Elder," Wiley says.

He's been waiting for us. I don't know how he got here or what he's been doing, but his clothes have seen better days, and his face is stained with drops of what appears to be his own blood.

"Good to see you kids alive," he tells us. "Are you ready for this?"

"Ready for what?" Maia asks him. "You never told us the rest of your plan."

"Rafe hasn't explained it to you yet?" asks the Elder.

"I had only just begun," Rafe says sheepishly. "It was a bit of a bumpy ride. Had to make sure we got here first, you know."

"Yes, well, we have little time now," the Elder says, his words coming out quick and focused. "But first, I want you all to meet my guest…"

The passenger door slowly opens from the truck the Elder had been waiting in when we arrived. A short figure in raggedy prison clothes appears from the shadows. I can't believe it.

"Father!" I yell, jumping out of my seat and through the back gate. "Father, you're alive! I thought you might have…"

"Niko!" he cries, embracing me, his arms thin and weak. He's fragile, even compared to the rest of us. "You made it. You made it. I'm so proud of you."

"What are you doing here?" I ask him. "How did…"

"It was the plan from the beginning," the Elder interrupts. "You must understand now why I didn't tell you. We couldn't afford for you to be distracted from your own part of the mission. I know you would have insisted on coming with me, but I needed you to assist Wiley without your mind on other things."

I don't care anymore. All that we've been through to get here. None of it matters now. My father is alive, but weak, and I must get him to safety.

"I am so happy to see you, Niko," my father tells me, his hands quaking as he holds himself up by my shoulder. "I didn't know if my eyes would have such joy again in this life. But we have no time to bask in this moment. The Elder has informed me of his plans and we must continue this course while we still have time."

"I understand, father," I tell him, though I wish it weren't true. I had not been in his presence, except for when we awaited the gallows, since the State stole us from the streets. "But what is the rest of the plan?"

"First we must wait," the Elder tells us. "But not long now. The minutes are winding down before the media gets word of what has happened at the prison."

"The media is run by the State," Maia says. "They're going to cover this up like everything else. They'll say they were running a drill undone by a technical malfunction."

"They can't cover this up," says the Elder. "This wasn't a small group of escapees fleeing toward the border. It was the entire prison. Yes, many of them were quickly contained, but the others are still in the streets and hills, wandering around, some looking for freedom, others for trouble. Remember, they weren't all among the Faithful."

"But the media will still take the State's side of things, won't they?" I ask. "That's who pays them. And they don't want to be the next ones to end up like us."

"Of course they will," says the Elder. "But they still have to ask the questions for the State to answer, and the President will have to come up with an answer, so the people will know what has happened."

"But the people always believe the State," Maia complains. "They blind their eyes to the truth because they see what they want to see and hear what they want to hear."

"That's where we come in," says the Elder. "We need to make the people see what they have become. They must know what the State has been hiding from them, give them a chance to change, to see the truth."

"How do you know it will work?" Maia asks.

"I don't," the Elder says. "But this is where my life among the Faithful has brought me, and it is all I can do to make up for my failure."

"Look," Rafe says. "Here they come! I've never seen the media swarm in like this, not even on Independence Day. I didn't know they had so many reporters."

"The State has never needed to cover themselves for something so big," the Elder says. "The earthquake that freed you kids, that was an act they could not have controlled. It was the planet revolting against them. But this…this was a security breach they allowed to happen right under their noses. The State, in their arrogance, has gotten lazy. That's how I knew we could beat their system. Now they'll need to answer to the citizens. The word of a prison break has certainly filled the streets."

"What do we do now?" I ask. "What's our plan?"

"We wait until it's our time," says the Elder. "Look now, the media is all surrounding a stage set on the front lawn. A microphone is placed in front of a podium. And now…look…the President is making his way toward the stage with his bodyguards. He will be making a hastily written speech. He will condemn our acts, tell the world of our evils, and assure the people that they are getting things quickly under control."

"And what are we going to do about it?" I ask.

"Time to walk," my father says. He had been quiet this entire time, and I am quickly reminded of how he always led. He has never been one to waste words, always waiting for his turn to speak, then he would get straight to the point.

"We're not going to bust our way through?" I ask.

"We'd be dead before we got to the gate," the Elder scoffs. "No, we aren't going near that mess. We're headed over the hill where we will be out of sight."

It is only now that I see the wisdom of the Elder's plan. We were never going to overrun the Capitol and push the President out of the way to get our message to the people. They have too many guards, too much protection. We never would have gotten through the gate.

Instead, we begin a short walk to a line of trucks that had just arrived, filled with broadcasting equipment powerful enough to reach the entire world. The media have all made their way to relay the President's address.

"Wiley, do you have anything…let's say…discreet?" asks the Elder.

"I have just the thing," Wiley responds with a smile, surely as relieved as I am that we aren't storming the castle. "What's our target?"

"The big white one with the large antenna on top," Rafe interjects. "It'll take me a minute to get into the system, but it's the only one strong enough to get our signal as far as we need it to go."

Wiley doesn't waste any time. He quickly slides a small device out of his pack, slips it onto a side door, and watches as it makes a tiny spark and falls off.

"That was easy," Wiley says. "Get in, brother."

Rafe slides the door open and hops into a chair that operates a command center reminiscent of the one underneath the prison. His hands work deftly and smartly as I witness him manipulate screens and dials while the rest of us pack in behind him.

I look into the Elder's face and see a man who is ready, but I'm not sure how he plans to convince the entire world that the same group who just released hundreds of prisoners, and is now hacking into the government's media system, is a group worthy of their trust. I pray he's as ready as he thinks he is.

"We're in!" Rafe says, clapping his hands as we watch the screen flip back to us. We look awful. A group of escaped criminals, malnourished, worn thin by time and misadventure.

"Hello," says the Elder, his voice noticeably shaking for the first time since I met him. "My name is Darius Monroe."

Darius Monroe? I ask myself. That means…

"In some circles, I have been known as Bramm Coyle. To others, I am known as the Elder, he continued. "There was an era when I was considered the most trustworthy advisor to the President of the Ariel, Samuel Shah. But there became a time and place when I lost his trust. I told him that his actions were immoral and that it would hurt the people who counted on him the most. Thus began the persecution of what we call The Faithful, and whom they call traitors to the State. My friends and I are now left with a last desperate attempt to declare to you the truth of what we believe and why we have been persecuted these past ten years. Let me start by…"

His speech is instantly cut off by a loud crack slamming through the side of the truck we have been sitting in. Blood splatters everywhere. We all dive to the floor immediately, except for one of us, the Elder, who has been shot in the center of his forehead, and is now lying dead on the dashboard, the console now disconnected from the media's broadcasting system.

"Cease fire!" can be heard over a megaphone. "Cease fire Immediately!"

The truck door slides open from the outside. "Out now!" shouts one of the president's officers. "Move! I won't tell you again."

Maia, closest to the door, crawls out. Her body sliding out like gelatin, exhausted, splattered by the Elder's blood.

"We're unarmed!" my father shouts, his lips dripping with an unfortunate truth. Wiley used his last explosive to get us inside.

"That's my truck!" yells out a man with a deep baritone voice. I can't see anything except a group of bodies frozen to the floor of the truck. My father puts his hands up. We've been through this before, but this was our last shot at freedom. We're only delaying the inevitable by days, maybe hours. We're as good as dead.

"What if there had been innocents in there?" shouts a woman with a microphone. "Who is responsible for opening fire without warning?"

"When did this become a war zone?" shouts another man. "You could have killed one of us!"

"These are dangerous criminals!" barks an officer, his gun still drawn at Felicity, her slender frame still holding her hands over her ears from the loud shot that killed the Elder as she creeps out of the side of the truck.

I'm in the back. I'll be the last one out, and I have little time, but I can't help but think about what the Elder just told the world. He said his name was Darius Monroe. That is no coincidence. My father trusted that man more than anyone. Could he…yes, he must have been…

Rafe and Wiley look into each other's eyes and nod. They know. They did everything they could. They're responsible for getting us this far, but it wasn't enough. They work their way to the open door with their hands raised and their eyes stricken with disgust.

"What were you doing in there?" someone shouts, but it couldn't have been an officer. They know why we were in there. They were alerted faster than we could have imagined. I don't know how they found us. They must have noted the same antennae we did. I do know why they shot. And I can't let this go. I have the last chance to fulfill the plan.

"Are you the escapees from Independence Day?" another asks.

"Of course they are!" shouts another. "Just look at them!"

"I don't remember hearing of an older one," says the man with a baritone voice.

"Is that a dead man inside?" asks another journalist. I can hear the murmur getting louder. More of the media circle us. "They killed someone! That could have been anyone!"

The media members, with their microphones on and cameras rolling, begin to shout down the officer who must have made the mortal shot. They don't know how many of us were in here. They don't know I'm still in here. The officers are distracted. This is my only opportunity.

I open a back window and slide myself through it without anyone looking my way. I climb up to the top of the truck and stomp loudly on the roof.

"My name is Niko Monroe!" I shout.

Suddenly every weapon within a quarter-mile of the news truck was aimed directly at me.

"You can't shoot him!" yells a member of the media. "He's unarmed!"

"This isn't justice!" yells another. "This is murder! That could have been any one of us in that truck!"

I stomp again.

"My name is Niko Monroe!" I shout louder. "You know my name, and you know my face, but you only know the part of the story the State wants you to hear!"

"Silence, traitor!" shouts an officer with his gun still pointed at me, despite others lowering theirs, fearing the media will turn on them. They don't mind killing us, but they don't want to be shown doing it on every news station in the State.

"I will no longer be silent as you attempt to bring us to the end of our lives!" I shout. "You have labeled us traitors, but we are not! We have committed no treason, we have not murdered, we have not robbed, we have done nothing but believe in a God who has commanded us to live in peace with all men!"

"You lie!" yells an officer.

"Do I lie?" I ask the crowd, with dozens of microphones and cameras pointed in my direction. "Is that what President Shah has declared? That we are traitors? If so, how? By asking for fairness? By asking for peace? By preaching how all people can find peace in a God of redemption? Our words were never told in secret. We have always been a people of love and kindness, living only in the fear of the God who made us all."

"Come down here, now!" shouts the officer. "You are under

arrest!"

"You can arrest me when I'm done speaking!" I shout over the murmur of the crowd. "I plead with you, those of you seeing this in your homes and offices. Do not forget my words. All we want is the same freedom we were promised from the beginning, and no one has freedom as long as the State is corrupt! We were all a people of freedom at one point in time, but you see before you men and women condemned to death only for a thought, a belief, for words that might convince everyone to turn away from corruption in the government. Search your hearts! What if they came for you next?"

I feel a sudden jolt of electricity bursting through my body. I fall limp into the arms of Wiley and Rafe, who were quick to catch me. It's over. Officers surround us and place us in handcuffs. We are rushed by reporters as they hound our captors with questions about their methods during our arrest, where they are taking us, and what they are going to do with us when we get there.

But we know the answer. Maybe they'll execute us in the gallows as originally planned. Maybe they'll throw us off the nearest cliff. I just hope my words reached someone.

We are quickly tossed in the back of a military police truck. It's dark, cold, and silent. No words are left to comfort one another. Only exhausted embraces and tears prayerfully offered to our God.

The ride is long and bumpy. By the time we arrived, I'm dehydrated and starving, but food and water won't be coming our way. I am tossed alone in a cell. No guard visitation, no threats, no beatings, just me left to wait, wonder, and pray until I pass out on the floor.

I have no sense of time in this place. I'm freezing, but I have no blanket to warm me. My body is weak with no nourishment to come. Am I forgotten? Am I left here to fade away until I meet the King?

I hope I am found, but I am losing consciousness. I hope there are others out there like us, except for our bonds. I pray for faith as I slip into the comfort of eternal sleep.

My eyes open and I see a bright light shining in my face. This isn't eternity. I know because everything hurts. Breathing is difficult. I feel a pinch in my arm. I see some liquid as it's fed into my body. I want to ask what's happening, but I can't speak.

"You're going to be okay," I hear from a familiar voice. My eyes open a little wider and see Maia standing at my side. "You were the last of us to be found. But we're all safe now."

Everyone except for the Elder, I think to myself, but I don't know how any of us are alive. I want to ask her a thousand questions, but my throat feels like it has been filled with sand for a week.

"It's a miracle you survived," she tells me. "You went days without food or water. These tubes feeding you are all that's kept you alive since you were found. You've been in a coma since sometime before the rescues began. I guess you don't know about any of that, though, do you? We have a lot of catching up to do."

I look at her and try to gesture to the door. It's the only way I can think to ask.

"Yes, your father is alive, but he is very sick," she says. "He wants to speak with you when you are both able. The others are in better shape, but no one is without injury or illness."

Maia grabs for a cup of water and slowly drips the cool liquid past my lips. I've never felt such relief. I close my eyes and try to relax. I try to speak again, but my lungs are heavy, my muscles have little life in them.

She goes on to tell me about how my words reached through the entire world. The media everywhere was incensed at how we had been treated, pleading ignorance in regards to their participation in such events. Foreign heads called for our release. The people were dismayed by their own actions, having rejoiced at our executions, falling for the deception that the State had convinced them to believe for so many years.

President Shah was ousted from his position. The Faithful are no longer outlawed from speaking the truth, and have won over a small number of believers, though most citizens were now merely tolerant of our existence. Some still hold onto the hatred they had built for so long, hoping our downfall is still coming.

"We're free to be ourselves," Maia tells me. "But for how long I do not know. When you have regained your strength, we will meet with the others. We're all proud of you, but we have much work left to do."

At least we now have hope.

May this letter bring you a greater understanding of our past, and peace if darker days do come again. Though we face dangers greater than ourselves, we are never alone.

The King will guide your path,

Niko Monroe, son of Hobbes Monroe the Wise, son of Darius Monroe the Elder, son of Niko the Brave, son of Jack Monroe the

Great. Peace be with you all.

Chapter Fifteen

Christmas

Jack's eyes opened, but his body was frozen, unable to move. Dawn was breaking, and snow had begun to fall on the ground outside once more. Somehow he was sweating profusely and didn't know what to make of it as he tried to gain his composure.

"What? How?" Jack began to mutter to himself, his voice unstable, his mind and body failing to adjust to his return to his new room, the attic he had spent the past several days cleaning, safe and sound where he belonged all along.

"There you are," his father said after poking his head up through the hole in the floor. "All that work cleaning and moving must have worn you out. You've been sleeping all day!"

"I don't feel like I slept at all," Jack groaned, his eyes attempting to blink through the crust. "What day is it?"

"What day is it?" his father repeated. "It's Christmas Eve, Jack. How long did you think you were out? You surely wasted the day away, as your mother and I decided you had earned a little rest, but there's still time for…"

"Christmas lights!" Jack jumped up, his legs suddenly recovering from their stupor. "Is it…is it time to go?"

"Everyone's waiting for you," his father said, his patience stronger than most days of the year. "Actually, that's why…"

"I'll get my coat," Jack interrupted, brushing past his father as he tried to remember where he had put it. "I can't believe I almost slept through the whole thing."

"That's the thing about sleep," his father thought out loud. "Everyone needs it, but we have it so we can get up and do something with our lives."

Jack wrinkled his eyebrows, but for once he didn't argue with his father, nor did he complain about the lecture. Instead, he considered the matter while hurriedly throwing his coat over his slender body.

"I really need to get a heater up here or something," Jack said as he followed his father down the stairs. "I woke up so cold I could hardly move. At least, that's what I think the problem…"

"Yes, yes," his father assured him. "Day after Christmas I'll go down to the store and get started on that. Unless you want to do it yourself?"

"I can drive the pickup?" Jack said with a giant grin.

"No," his father deadpanned. "I meant…"

"Merry Christmas Eve!" his mother welcomed them as she opened the front door. "At least what's left of it. Are you going to be able to sleep tonight? Or were you planning on waiting all night for…"

"I don't know if I'll ever sleep again," Jack answered quickly. "I… I…well, never mind that, where are we going this year?"

"You can't be serious?" Calvin asked him. His little brother took Christmas light viewings more seriously than anything else in his young life.

"Why can't I be serious?" Jack scoffed at Calvin's accusations. "I've been a little busy the past few days, cleaning up that junkyard upstairs. And we go somewhere different every year, so why would I know where we're going?"

"Because everyone in town knows about the Jasper Lights Festival opening this year," said Samantha. "The whole town has been working on it for weeks. Sometimes I wonder where your mind goes."

"It's gonna be awesome!" said Sadie.

"It's at San…San…Sanniko's!" Calvin stammered.

"Saint Nicholas' Farms," Samantha corrected him.

"Right," Calvin said. "San Niko's Farms, just like I said. It's supposed to have every style of Christmas light imaginable."

"Then what are we waiting for?" Jack asked. "Let's get to San Niko's before it's too late."

"I want to sing Christmas carols!" Sadie squealed.

"Me too, me too!" Samantha giggled.

"I want to see the Christmas tree!" Calvin shouted louder than was necessary. "I hear it's gonna be bigger than the one I saw on television!"

But Jack followed slowly behind with his father.

"Dad?" Jack asked.

"What is it?" his father replied as Jack's brother and sisters rushed into the backseat of their minivan. "Are you hungry?"

"No, it's not that..." Jack said softly. "Well, yes, I could go for a sandwich or something, but I was just wondering...can you tell me more about grandpa? One of the maps in the attic was...ummm... curious. Can you tell me more about what he wanted to do with them?"

"We'll talk about it on the way," his father said, putting his arm on Jack's shoulder. "But the story of those maps does not begin with him."

Jack nodded and asked his mother if he could sit in the front seat next to his father. She shrugged and agreed and the Monroe family was soon off to begin their night of festivities.

Calvin witnessed the biggest Christmas tree he would see until he was a very old man. Samantha and Sadie sang louder than the rest of the carolers combined. The children all played games, ran around in a light layer of snow, and took several rides on a Christmas train the town had set up to go around the entire farm.

That night, they each slept soundly in their own beds, even Jack. He had to bundle up quite snugly, of course, but he knew his father would take care of his little heating problem soon enough.

Christmas morning came and went just the same as any other for the Monroe family. Presents were shared, movies played, and the fire kept them nice and toasty as Joshua Monroe retold the story of a King born in a manger. His mother made cinnamon rolls and they went perfectly with hot cocoa in the green and red mugs they had received in their stockings.

Christmas was the same as it always had been for the Monroe family, but the eldest child was quite different. Jack knew he would never be the same and that this was only the beginning of something greater to come.

THE END

CPSIA information can be obtained
at www.ICGtesting.com
Printed in the USA
BVHW032116081220
595227BV00023B/364